Faith in the Flesh

The First Law
From Bad Flesh

Tim Lebbon

To Trev, Lorraine & Jonathan

To the sexiest... you know the rest!

love from Tim 7/11/98

RAZORBLADE PRESS

This book was first published in 1998 by
RazorBlade Press, 186 Railway St, Splott, Cardiff,
CF2 2NH.

Designed and typeset by
RazorBlade Press and John Phelps

Printed and bound in the U.K by Redwood Books,
Trowbridge.

British Library in Publication Data.
A catalogue record for this book is available
from the British Library

ISBN 0-9 531468-4-7

Also by the same author:

Mesmer

Shortlisted for the 1998 British Fantasy Award for best novel.

"a firm and confident style, with elements of early Clive Barker" *Phil Rickman, Radio Wales*

"Mesmer is absolutely superb. Lebbon's going to be big one day. Start reading him now." *Simon Clark*

"Mesmer is an excellent taster from a new writer." *SFX*

"Mesmer is beatifully written, with Lebbon timing the fireworks to perfection" *Zene*

published by Tanjen ISBN 1901530027

Faith in the Flesh

To my brother and sisters:
Nick, Catherine, Iz & Joan, for a million good reasons

I would like to thank the following people for their encouragement and advice, and for ensuring that writing is not a lonely business: Allen Ashley, Anthony Barker, Simon Clark, Mat Coward, Pete Crowther, Darren Floyd, Gary Greenwood, Marni Griffin, Rhys Hughes, Des Lewis, Steve Lockley, Max O'Hagan, Katherine Roberts, Mark Samuels, John Travis, Gavin Williams and Matt Williams.

Introduction

By Peter Crowther

Not every writer can tell a story and not every storyteller can write.

Why? Here's why:

Writing fiction is not simply a matter of stringing together a few words until they make a sentence, and then stacking a few sentences on top of the one you've just finished until you've filled a page. It's about thinking about your audience, thinking about the way you'd tell the story to them if they were sitting around you...maybe late at night, out in the countryside miles away from anywhere, plopped down cross-legged around a crackling fire after a hard day's walking and a big meal and maybe a couple of beers, with the dancing flames making the shadows move behind the barrier of trees beyond the furthest tent.

You'd say to them. 'Here's how it started...' and you'd maybe shuffle yourself around a little, leaning closer so the fire's glow plays across your eyes. Then, after checking the faces of your audience to make sure they're with you (or at least, prepared to *join* you), you'd carry on.

A lot of writers don't seem to do that. Either they're not able to or they simply can't be bothered to make the effort.

But Tim Lebbon does. Maybe he's been doing it all his life.

When I was asked to take a look at a couple of Tim's novella manuscripts prior to publication, I have to confess I hadn't come across his work before. But then I read the single-line first paragraph of 'The First Law' and I knew I was onto a good thing:

On their fifth day adrift at sea, they saw an island.

What!? Five days adrift at sea? Why was that? What had happened? Who are these people? And why does the discovery of this island sound like it's not going to wind up being good news?

I was hooked. I wanted — *needed* — to know the answers to these questions, fully realising that there would be other questions that would need to be answered before we were through. Right away, I was leaning closer to that campfire, forgetting whatever it was I had been doing and concentrating only on getting some answers. Somehow, I just knew from that opening line that we were in for a rocky ride. What I didn't know was just how rocky the ride was going to be.

Tim Lebbon is a teller of stories, a raconteur who happens to be able to spin his yarn on printed page. He has a grasp on language and description and characterisation, and he has an understanding of the dual concept of pace and timing. Better than that, though he has a wild imagination...as the two long tales which follow eloquently demonstrate.

'The First Law' calls to mind — without plagiarising — Robert E Howard's wonderful imagery of apparently-deserted monolithic structures in which Conan always used to think it was safe to get out of the desert wind for a while! If you bemoan the fact that nobody seems to be writing stuff to rival William Hope Hodgson's THE HOUSE ON THE BORDERLAND or Clark Ashton Smith's tales of the doomed lands of Zothique, Hyperborea, Poseidonis and Xiccarph, you're going to weep with joy. And if you regard Fritz Leiber's 'A Bit Of The Dark World' as something of a watershed in unrelentingly dark fiction, you're in for a pleasant hour or so.

Like the very best work from all those wordsmiths of atmospherically-charged epics of densely described prose hinting at but never detailing swirling, doom-laden menace, 'The First Law' progresses slowly and effortlessly, pulling us along with it as we learn of the arrival of five shipwrecked men on an island which is, to say the least, pretty inhospitable.

In the pages that follow, discoveries, mysteries, accidents, incidents and fatalities dog the men's slow and tortuous climb to the island's mountainous middle-ground from where they hope to see exactly where they are. As they trudge wearily and despondently through a maze of bizarre flora and fauna the men encounter a variety of creatures (most of which seem uninterested in their presence...)while attempting to preserve their strength and energy by sampling some of the bizarre fruits along the way. Needless to say, the fruits don't do most of the things they should...and pretty much everything they shouldn't and the men begin to lose their hold on reality.

Then things start to go bad.

And that's only the first story.

For those of you who turn, head shaking, to the next tale expecting even the briefest respite, let me warn you now: there is nowhere to hide in this book. Nowhere to catch your breath. Nowhere to duck out of the literary storm conjured up by Lebbon.

The Wyndam-esque post-apocalyptic 'From Bad Flesh' is a sombre and off-kilter piece set on a near-future Earth devastated by a terrible plague. We join the terminally-ill protagonist as he sets out across inhospitable, empty vastnesses covered in scabby, suppurating sores, dodging the harmful rays of the sun, bands of murderous outlaws and occasional lakes composed entirely of putrefying corpses (some of whom are still trashing...), in search of a fabled cure and the strange man who might be able to supply it.

Yep, not a lot of laughs here either.

But then you're not here for laughs, are you? You're here to be told tales, and maybe, to be unsettled. Well, you've come to the right place.

So pull up that branch. Throw a couple of logs on the fire and park yourself a while. Ignore the rustling from the trees and listen: Tim Lebbon's going to weave some word-magic. And the chances are you're going to like it so much, you're not going to let him stop for a long, long time.

Peter Crowther
Harrogate, July 1998.

The First Law

"*Self-presevation is the first law of nature.*"
proverb

"*What a book a devils chaplain might write on the clumsy, wasteful, blundering, low and horribly cruel works of nature.*"
Charles Darwin.

1. THE DEVIL'S CHAPLAIN

On their fifth day adrift at sea, they saw an island.

At first, there were only teasing hints of land: a twisted clump of palm fronds; darting specks in the sky which may have been birds; a greenish tinge to the underside of the soft clouds in the north, just above the horizon. They should have felt impelled to paddle towards it, but five days of sun, thirst and heat had drained them of hope. They lay slumped in the boat, their skin red and blistered, tongues swollen, lips split and black with dried blood.

Their ship had been torpedoed and sunk five days earlier. So far as they knew, they were the only survivors. They had begun to feel cursed, not blessed.

"I think there's an island there," Butch said, "unless the clouds are green with envy." He was small, normally chipper, and one side of his face was badly bruised from the sinking. He knelt at the front of the lifeboat and stared out across the sea, a grotesque figurehead.

Roddy closed his eyes against the blazing sun, but still the light found its way through. It was as though his eyelids were turning transparent through lack of sustenance. The lifeboat had been capsized when they found it, and any supplies previously stored on board had been swallowed by the sea. On the third day it had rained, and they had managed to trap enough water in cupped hands and bundled clothes for a few mouthfuls each. Since then, they had gone thirsty. Roddy felt life seeping from his body with every drop of sweat.

Ernie was the only officer with them, but fortunately he had refused to pull rank. He seemed to acknowledge, as they all did, that their position levelled anything so fleeting as grade. They had all been thrown together by the disaster of war, into the same class-- that of survivor. So he prayed out loud instead, and at first his praying had helped, until Roddy had commented on how prayers had not aided the other 300 of the ship's crew. Since then, Ernie had been sitting at the stern, spouting occasional brief worshipful outbursts as if to goad the others into violence.

It was not that Roddy had no sense of religion. It simply felt redundant out here, in the middle of the ocean. Today, he thought, God was indifferent.

"Definitely an island," Butch said. "Look. Leaves, or something. Covered in bird shit, too."

Roddy managed to raise his head, then his upper body, until he was sitting up. Joints creaked in protest, he moaned in sympathy. His stomach felt huge and heavy and swollen. Ironic, seeing as he had not eaten for days. The sun beat at his forehead like a white-hot sledgehammer, trying to mould him all out of shape. He looked in the direction Butch was indicating and saw an island of dead things floating by. But among the brown leaves, several huge egg shapes clung on with wispy tenacity.

"Coconuts," he said.

"Must be migrating," Butch commented.

Norris, apparently asleep until now, raised his hairy head. "Do they migrate?"

"Stupid bastard," Butch muttered, to himself more than to Norris. The need for survival may have thrown them together, but it could not change the way they thought of the cook. He was unliked and unlikeable. He had been on three ships which had sunk in the past year, and if anyone attracted the badge of Jonah, it was Norris. He took any such suggestion to heart and fought the man who made it, but this only drove the gossip underground and made it harsher.

"Shut your mouth, Norris," Ernie said. "Of all the people God could choose to put on our boat of survivors--"

"I put myself here, mate," Butch cut in.

"Of all the people," Ernie continued, unabated, "we get you."

Norris sat up and winced. "What do you mean by that, you trumped-up shit?" His lips were bleeding. Skin had sloughed from his burnt forehead, and now hung down over his eyes. Roddy wondered vaguely whether it helped to keep the sun at bay, and almost put his hand up to his own forehead to see whether he was in the same state.

"He means," said Max, "that you're a Jonah. A curse, a bad omen. You're the ancient mariner, and you wear our lives around your scrawny neck."

"Ancient! You're the ancient one, you old bastard. Look at you, big and bald..."

Norris trailed off when he saw that nobody was listening anymore. Butch was banging on the gunwale with the palm of his hand, trying to attract their attention. Max stood in the centre of the boat, and Roddy marvelled once again at his resilience. He was over six feet tall, big without being fat, bald as a baby and about as mild-mannered. The wrong man for a war, Roddy had always maintained. Max was intelligent, educated and sensitive, and Roddy had seen him cry more than once. He was also one of the bravest men Roddy knew. But his was a bravery gained by confronting his fears and grabbing them by the throat, not by blindly rushing a machine-gun emplacement without a second thought. The latter bordered more on foolishness, in Roddy's book. Max was brave because he would never let his fears defeat him.

"Now I see it," Max said.

Butch stood as well, but became annoyed when he could not see the island.

"Sit down, shorty," Max growled. "I'm lookout for the next couple of hours."

"All heart, you are." Butch sat but continued staring forward, as if willing the island into view.

By now it was obvious that the tides, winds and fate were carrying them towards the land hidden below the horizon. The ceiling of clouds reflected dull green, giving them a tantalising glimpse of what the island may contain. Hours passed. The sea lifted, tilted and dipped them closer. Ernie sat at the stern and gave thanks to God. Hope had begun to bleed into their thoughts, reviving them, aggravating hunger and thirst with the contemplation of their possible assuagement on the island. Ernie prayed, and they all heard and wanted to believe him. Maybe God had been watching them, guiding them on their way with a wave of his hand, steering them towards the island, and salvation.

As darkness began to fall, and the land slowly emerged out of the sea, Roddy felt an emptiness inside. It was as if he were looking at a nothing, a physical manifestation of the void in his beliefs. He tried to thank God, but found his thoughts as cold and as empty as the island before him appeared to be.

He looked around at his companions. None of them seemed inclined to paddle to reach land any quicker. It was as if they were all enjoying these final, brief moments cast aimlessly adrift.

The sounds from the island hurt their senses.

After five days at sea, with little more than the soporific waves and their own voices to listen to, the cacophony of the breaking waters was almost unbearable. Half a mile out from the island, the sea smashed into a barely visible reef, turning white and violent. Their boat nudged its way through a toothless gap, as though guided in by a helping hand, and Ernie sat with his eyes closed and his mouth working, prayers tumbling forth like bodies from a sinking ship. Spray from the disturbed sea swept across the boat and soaked them. Roddy could not help opening his mouth and tasting the water; salt stung his dried and split lips, and the bitter taste of the sea drained once more into his throat.

"Thank God," Norris said, and Ernie agreed.

"Can't wait to meet the native women," Butch called dryly.

"Thought you had a missus at home," Max shouted.

"At home, yes," Butch said with a nod, and Roddy could not help but laugh at his semi-serious expression. His laughter was short-lived. This was not the place for it, and they all felt that; silence reigned once more. Merriment did not sit right with the roar of the surf behind them.

When the boat nudged onto the beach, Roddy felt a sick lurch in his guts. Everything was suddenly real, solid, and he noticed the pattern of grain in the wood of the boat for the first time. He saw how some of the oar mountings had begun to rust and dribble a red stain onto the timber. He could feel the tightness of his shoes, the abrasiveness of their insides as though they were already full of sand. He was even aware of his own body, in more detail than at any time during the past five days: his bruised left elbow, where he had struck it jumping from the burning and sinking ship; the splinters in his hands and forearms, from his struggle to turn the capsized lifeboat upright; even the weight of his thoughts and memories. He thought of Joan, his girlfriend back home, and realised that she had barely entered his mind since the sinking. Now, with the possibility of survival thoughts of Joan were flashing back. Her willing smile, bottle-green eyes, generous nature. A hard, bitter kiss on the day he had left her to go to war. For a while, he had thought that she blamed him. But her anger, he knew, was directed elsewhere, at an unfairness impossible to personify. Her bitterness had stayed with him, transferred in the kiss.

The island was reminding him of who he was.

Butch climbed from the boat and fell drunkenly to his knees on the wet sand. Max followed suit, then Norris, who staggered further along the beach. He was staring at a point beneath the palm trees skirting the sands.

"Come on," Roddy said to Ernie. The officer remained at the stern of the boat, unresponsive, rocking with the gentle movements of the lagoon. "Ernie!"

Ernie's eyes blinked to life. Moisture replaced their dark sheen. "God brought us here," he said, but it sounded more like a challenge than a statement.

"Yes, sir, He did," Roddy said, though he doubted any truth in the words. His faith, drummed into him by his parents and teachers, had deserted him and left an aching void, which could only be penetrated by the truth. "God brought us here."

"But why?" Ernie stood and walked unsteadily along the boat, pausing at the grounded bow. He looked down at the sand, staring at the smudged footprints of the others already on the beach. Then he glanced back at Roddy, and his voice was distorted. "Why?"

"Why what?" Roddy asked, but the officer was climbing from the boat, stepping gingerly as if afraid that he would sink at any moment.

Roddy followed. He felt a moment of disorientation, so used was he to the constant movement of the boat. His stomach lurched as it tried to maintain the motion, then settled again. The sand was warm, even through his shoes.

Norris had wandered along the beach, while the others waited in the shadow of palm trees. Leaves hung from the high branches, pointing down at the men like the wings of great sleeping bats.

Roddy fell to his knees with the others, wondering why he did not feel at all liberated. "At least it seems pretty verdant," he said. "Where there are palms, there's water, and birds, and animals. Fruit too. Food and water. Safety."

Butch frowned and stared out to sea, his eyes revealing a strange longing for the terrible five days just gone by. His face was bleeding again but he seemed not to notice. Flies began to buzz around him, as though he were dead.

"Butch?" Roddy said. He did not like seeing the little man so quiet. It was unnatural, disconcerting in the extreme. "Butch? What say we go and find the native women?"

"Doubt there are any," Butch said. His gaze never faltered; he wanted to avoid looking back at the island for as long as possible. "This place feels dead."

His words made Roddy, already chilled by his sunburn, shiver. It was a strange statement, especially coming from Butch, but it seemed so right. Roddy tried to shake the words, but they were spoken, and now they held power. "Max?" he said, searching for something. Comfort, perhaps.

Max looked at him long and hard. Roddy had known him for a long time, and he had never seen a look like this. He knew that Max was vaguely superstitious, but he had never actually seen him afraid of something he could not see. Max's superstition was like the trace of his own religion, in that it was inbred rather than self-propagated--handed down through generations, instead of defined and created through personal experience. Even though Max was a thinker, some things were planted too deep to think around.

"We make our own Hell," Max said.

"What the fuck is that supposed to mean?" Butch exploded, digging his hands into the sand.

Max shrugged. "It just seemed to sound right. This place feels all wrong. We'll have to be careful."

"How can a place be wrong?" Roddy asked. Max was frightening him, badly.

"It's God's place," Butch said, imploring Ernie to back him up. "Isn't it, sir? God's own place, and He's saved us from dying on the sea." His hands had closed tight, and sand flowed between his fingers like sacrificial blood.

"I'm sure God doesn't know a thing about this place," Ernie said. He turned and looked past the palm trees, to the rich wall of foliage blocking any view further inland.

"Bollocks!" Roddy said. Hiding his fear. Becoming angry so that he could not dwell on what he was really feeling, the jaws of doubt even now gnawing at his bones. "Crap. Get your act together, you lot. We've got to find water, food and shelter. Norris!" He stood and called along the beach to where the cook was rooting around by a fallen tree.

"There's something blowing bubbles in the sand," Norris shouted back.

"Come here, we've got to start getting ourselves together," Roddy said, but then he felt his knees beginning to betray him, and he fell onto his rump in the sand. As he slumped slowly onto his back, a hand caught his head and eased it down. Nausea overtook him, then a swimming fatigue that worked to swallow him whole. As his eyelids took on a terrible weight he tried to see the first stars. He had an awful feeling that he would not recognise any of the constellations, but the palm trees hid them from view anyway, and darkness blanked his mind.

He was not really unconscious. Everything moved away for a while: noises coming from an echoing distance, sensations of heat and pain niggling like bad memories. Voices mumbled dimly, words unrecognizable. He felt the cool kiss of water on his lips, sudden and sweet, and he opened his mouth and glugged greedily.

"Steady," Max said. "Not too much." He was kneeling above him, twisting his shirt so that drops fell into Roddy's mouth.

"Fresh?" Roddy asked.

Max nodded. "There's a stream further along the beach." His face was grim and he said no more, but Roddy felt too tired to pursue the subject.

The five of them sat where they had landed for an hour, taking turns to walk to the stream and soak their shirts in fresh water. Max had made a half-hearted search for a smashed coconut to use as a cup, but had found none. There was little talk, but the attitude of the men spoke volumes. Ernie had stopped praying.

When Roddy's turn came to fetch the water he relished the time alone. He realised that he had experienced no privacy for five whole days, even relieving himself in front of the other men. The sea roared at the reef to his left, the silent shadowy island was a massive weight to his right, threatening at any moment to bear down and crush him into the sand. He tried not to look into the jungle, averting his gaze from darkness as he had as a child, struggling to convince himself that what he could not see did not exist. Even the silence seemed wrong. Where were the animals? Away from of his fellow survivors, his feeling of being watched was almost overwhelming.

When he reached the stream he eased himself to his knees and leant over the running waters. In the vague light of the clear night sky, he was a shadow. The water spilled and splashed past rocks holding out against time.

The banks were scattered with things carried down from further inland, and he tried to see what they were in the moonlight. A huge feather, tattered by whatever had torn it from its owner. A dead thing with many legs, as big as his hand and hairier. Something long and slinky, with oily scales glimmering in the silvery light and a dark smudge where a chunk had been taken from the body.

All bad things, Roddy thought. All dead. But was dead necessarily bad?

He soaked the shirts, stood and made his way back to his companions. They were silent, as before, but there was a tension between them which was almost visible. If he could see it, Roddy thought, it would be black and dead, like the things in the stream. He wondered whether his brief absence had allowed him to register it more certainly, as when one leaves a room and then notices its smell upon re-entering.

"At least there are animals," he said. "Something we can eat." Nobody answered. Max looked at him, but in the dark Roddy could not read his expression. He was glad.

They each took another drink, but the water tasted different now. Roddy thought of the dead things as he drank and it was all he could do to keep it down. It no longer smelt fresh, but rancid. It soothed his dried throat, however, and for tonight at least he did not care what harm it might do him.

They agreed to spend the night on the beach. They all lay out in the open, to prevent anything falling on them from the palm trees. Their breathing slowed and deepened until a sudden grinding, rasping sound jerked them all back from the verge of sleep.

"What the hell?" Butch called.

"His demons are come!" Ernie yelled.

"All mutations," Max muttered.

Roddy sat up and saw their lifeboat being sucked back out to sea. Whatever minimal currents there were had now turned, and the boat was drifting further and further away from the beach. In the moonlight, it was a nonchalant sea monster.

Shorn of their dreams, the men sat silently and watched.

"We could swim out and get it," Norris suggested. "It's our only hope."

"Go on then," said Butch. "Just tell us how to cook what's left of you, when you wash up on the beach."

"Could be anything in there," Max said. "Sharks. Jellyfish. Octopus."

"Creating your own hell?" Roddy asked, but regretted it at once. He was scaring himself as much as the others. Max stared at him darkly, as if trying to share a secret, or steal one back.

They all sat and watched the boat bob closer to one of the gaps in the reef. Roddy felt helpless and exposed. He recalled a time in his childhood when his mother had seen him off on a school trip. He had not wanted to go on his own, he so wanted her to come, but control was snatched from him totally the instant he boarded the bus. His mother waved and he wanted to wave back, but his arm seemed not to work. He could only cry as the bus pulled off, taking him further away from comfort and safety, hauling him towards whatever imagined doom those in charge deemed suitable for him. He had sensed that his life was run by others even then -- his mother, the teachers, the bus driver with his mass of hair yellowed by cigarettes -- and he had felt it again throughout his time in the navy. Sent here, ordered there, guided not by the hand of fate, but by the sadistic whims of war.

Never had his feeling of impotence been so strong as when he watched their boat drift away.

He felt an incredible emptiness inside as the boat was dashed to shadowy shards on the reef. Their last tenuous link with the outside world had been broken. Or rather, cut.

There was nothing they could do. The darkness seemed to inhibit conversation, so they soon slept again. As he finally drifted off, Roddy realised that he had not slept properly for over five days. The haunted silence of the island gave them the sensory peace they needed to sleep, though not restfully.

Crazy ideas floated in the nether regions of sleep: maybe the island wanted them gone for a while, so that it could do whatever it had to do? "All mutations," Max had muttered. Even mutants had need of food.

Sleep was waterlogged with dreams. Twisted images of violent waters corrupted with oil and refuse and blood, grumbling torpedoes slamming in to finish the job, limbs floating past fins, cries drowned, hope sinking away beneath them, pulling them down, sucking them into the dark. Roddy thrashed in the sand, working the grains into skin split by five days of sun, choking on it as he dreamt of teeth shattered by the pressures of deep water.

A voice came from the void, clear and high above the tormented sounds of hot metal warping and snapping. Its words were hidden but its meaning clear, the panic evident in its troubled tone. Thoughts, ideas and sentences flowed together into a collage of desperation. God was mentioned, prayed for and then discarded, with an outpouring of tears greater than the troubled world should ever allow.

Roddy surfaced from sleep like a submarine heading for the light. He saw a twitching shape along the beach: Ernie, jerking in his sleep as jumbled catechisms fell from his mouth to be muffled forever in the ageless sand. Pleas to God, and denials of Him in the same sentence. Faith in salvation and a piteous, hopeless resignation. It was horrible to hear because it was so senseless, and Roddy thought he should go and wake Ernie, drag him from whatever depths of nightmare he had sunken to.

But he was afraid. Scared that once he reached him, Ernie would already be awake, but still not free of the nightmare.

There were other noises around them in the dark, a background mumble and chitter from the island that had not been there when they first arrived. Secret things were happening. The whole place had been waiting for them to sleep before coming back to life.

Roddy glanced towards the jungle and saw a shape under the trees: a shadow within deeper shadows. It was a woman, naked and ravaged by disease, and she was holding out her hands, her mouth open in a silent scream. Joan, he thought, but it was not her. The tortured woman wanted to tell them something, but she could make no sound. As the palm fronds moved in the sea breeze, so her arms wavered, drifting in time to the shadows. Her jaw worked in synchronicity with the sea, and sighing waves mimicked the sounds she could not utter.

Then a cloud covered the moon and the image vanished into leaves and shadow.

Ernie muttered on. The sea stroked the land. More clouds passed overhead and clotted the moonlight, and as total darkness fell Roddy closed his eyes to hide from it.

"Get away! Get it away! Oh God, help him!"

"Kick it! Use a rock or something, kill it!"

Roddy was woken from monotone dreams to a bloody nightmare. Max and Butch were standing next to him, looking along the beach and shouting. He leapt to his feet and cringed as his wounds and burns reminded him of their existence.

Then all pain went. Feeling fled, replaced by a numbness of mind rather than body.

Ernie was lying in wet sand, but it was not wet from the sea. It was dark and cloggy, lumpy and glistening. A layer of flies flickered across its surface like a black sheet caught in a breeze: lifting, landing, lifting again. Ernie twitched redly in the morning sun. Something was eating him.

"Uh!" Roddy could not talk. He could hardly move, his legs cramping beneath him, but he was oblivious to the pain, hardly conscious of his spasming muscles.

The thing was huge and grey, its head darting out to snap delicate mouthfuls of flesh from Ernie's throat and face. Its body was almost as long as Ernie, who lay in a smear of his own blood. The thing glanced at them, expressing no fear or trepidation, its eyes lifeless black pearls in the thick probe of its head. It wore a shell like that of a giant tortoise scraped and scarred, patterned with smears of its breakfast's blood. The beach stank of aged dead things.

A series of thumps came from behind. Roddy spun around in terror. Norris dashed past him with a length of wood held high, a rusted iron fitting still visible on one edge. He hit the creature and fell back as the vibration jarred his arms.

"Come on!" Max shouted, running forward to help. He grabbed the length of splintered wood from the stunned Norris and smashed it down on the shell, careful not to strike the giant tortoise's head in case he drove it deeper into Ernie's face. His blow had no apparent effect. He turned the board over so that the iron fitting faced down, and brought it arcing over his head once more. This time the blow left a bright splash of scarred shell, urging Max to greater effort.

Butch had found a rounded stone the size of his hand and he threw it at the tortoise, retrieved it when it rebounded, threw it again.

The tortoise snapped another mouthful of raw flesh from Ernie's face. Roddy thought it may have been his nose.

He looked around for something to use as a weapon, but could see nothing. His heart was thumping in his chest, his tongue sandy and swollen and raw. He needed a piss.

Ernie was dead.

He stumbled over to a spot next to Max and kicked sand at the creature's head, spraying it across Ernie's flayed face in the process.

"Careful!" Norris shouted at him.

Roddy almost laughed. "He's dead," he said, still kicking, dodging the board when Max brought it down on the shell once more. The wood splintered and cracked, the heavy end dropping next to the tortoise's front legs.

The thing turned and left. They were all surprised at its speed as it hauled its weight up the beach and disappeared into the foliage beneath the trees.

"Bastard!" Butch shouted after it. Roddy had an unsettling feeling that it had left because it was full, not as a result of their ineffective attack. The way it had looked at them, as though they were little more than the trees it rubbed against as it retreated inland, had turned Roddy cold.

"Oh Jesus, where the hell have we ended up?" Butch gasped, stumbling backwards until he tripped over his own feet and fell onto his back. Humour was his defence mechanism, but sometimes even that could not work. Sometimes, things were beyond a joke. His hands were bleeding.

"Big tortoise," Norris remarked. "Make a hell of an ashtray."

"Shut up," Butch said, "just shut up, you bloody jinx. It's your fault we're here anyway; if you hadn't--"

"What?" Norris demanded.

Butch did not reply. He turned and stared out to sea, shaking, his grubby shirt pasted to his body with sweat. He licked blood from his hands and spat it at the sand. He looked like an animal, Roddy thought.

"Take a look," Max said, nodding at Ernie's ruined body.

Roddy shook his head, started to walk away. He had seen enough. He was not yet twenty-five, and he had seen a thousand dead men. Max grabbed his arm, and Roddy wondered once again what Max had meant last night: what were "all mutations"?

"Roddy, take a look," Max said again. Confidence was still there in his voice, though camouflaged beneath dull shock.

Ernie was a mess. His blood speckled the sand with spray patterns. Roddy tried to avoid looking at the face, because there was little left to see. He noticed a pulped book lying at the dead man's side, and wondered how the hell Ernie had kept his Bible through everything that had happened.

Then he saw the officer's left hand: wounded, the blood already dried and caked into a black mess. He looked at the right hand, bent and lifted the arm, just to make sure that what he was seeing was not imagination.

"Cut his wrists," Roddy said quietly.

"What?" Norris asked. Butch looked up.

Max turned and walked a few steps before sitting down, facing away.

"He slit his wrists," Roddy said. "In the night. Must have done it a while ago, the blood's already clotted." He spotted something glinting on the blood-soaked sand by Ernie's hip. He knew how useful a knife would be, but he could not bring himself to pick it up.

"God-fearing fool decides to off himself instead of facing up to what God had given him," Norris muttered. "We could live here for years, and he tops himself as soon as we're out of the sea."

"I heard him, I think," Roddy continued, trying to ignore Norris's dismissive tone of voice. "I woke up in the night. Half woke, anyway. He was mumbling, moaning. It wasn't very nice."

"What was he saying?" Butch asked. He was staring wide-eyed at the corpse now, as if he could more easily accept a death caused by the victim's own hand than by something unknown. In a way, Roddy admitted to himself, it wasn't as bad. It displayed a weakness in Ernie, rather than a strength in this unknown place.

"I didn't listen for long. I can't remember. I was tired. I was dreaming. I went back to sleep." Did I? Roddy thought quickly. Straight back to sleep? He glanced at the place where he had seen the shape beneath the trees, but there was nothing there.

Nobody said anything. Even Norris turned away and walked off towards the stream.

Roddy sat next to Max, who was making vague shapes in the sand.

"I think we should go inland," Max said sullenly. "See if there's any other signs of life here. Any human inhabitants."

"I don't think there will be," Roddy said, and Max did

2. INTO THE TREES

Roddy had expected a long, harrowing journey through dense jungle. Snakes dipping down from trees to kiss his shoulders. Spiders in his hair.

They were all equally surprised when, within five minutes, they emerged from the cover of trees onto a wide, undulating plain. The four men paused to rest and take in the view, their bodies weaker from their ordeal than they had at first thought. Hearts thumped, blood pumped through muscles jaded by five days of inactivity, hunger and thirst. Just as it had on the ocean, the sun continued its attack, relentless and indifferent. Burnt skin peeled and revealed the raw pinkness below to the heartless rays.

Roddy knelt on the ground and ran his hand through the rich grass. It looked almost like a meadow or hillside back home in Wales, but there were no daisies here, no dandelions. The grass felt sharper than it should, angry to the touch. It bent stiffly and sprang back with a rustle.

"Anyone for cricket?" Butch asked, but he received no reply, not even a rebuke. Instead, they walked out into the grassland.

Ernie was dead. So were the rest of the crew, but Ernie had been a survivor. He had been one of them, if only for five days. That length of time had set them apart from the rest of the ship's complement, and losing Ernie was like losing the ship all over again. Their hopes, however vague and troubled, seemed to have sunk with him. The men were silent. They walked immersed in their own worlds. Ernie was with all of them, in all their thoughts: either alive and spouting prayers, or dead and bleeding into the sand.

For Roddy, Ernie was still the gibbering shadow in the night, talking himself into a hopeless death while a shape moved under the trees, trying to scream. Roddy had not told the others of his hallucination. He put it down to hunger, but subconsciously there was something else there. Something with a pleading mouth and flayed, torn skin.

None of them had been able to say a prayer over Ernie's grave. Roddy hated that. He felt as if they had let Ernie and themselves down. God must not be too happy with them today.

Four pairs of feet whispered through the grass, kicking up angry puffs of insects. From the position of the sun Roddy could tell that they were moving north, towards the highest point they could see from here. He reckoned the mountain - hill, really -- to be a thousand feet high, its gentle lower slopes wooded, the higher parts splashed with clumps of colour like an artist's well-used palette. It was smooth-topped and well-worn by time, speckled with outcroppings of a dark, sharp rock. It dominated their view in one direction, hiding whatever lay beyond. In the other direction, west and south west, the grassland drifted away towards a hilly, heavily wooded area. Steam rose from this jungle, drifting straight up into the air until it was caught by an invisible breeze and condensed into wispy clouds. A few birds swung to and fro high above the island, rarely flapping their wings. They circled higher, swooped down, circled again. Roddy felt observed.

"This is a horrible place," Norris mumbled.

"Why so?" asked Max. His words sounded flat, as if he desired to hear other voices without caring what they said. Even Norris's voice.

"Don't know," Norris said shortly, as if to disappoint Max. They walked in silence for a while, then Norris spoke out once more. "Just feels horrible. Like a hillside before rain. Loaded."

"Loaded with your bad luck," Butch muttered, but for once Norris refrained from retorting.

"Where are we going?" Roddy asked. He looked back the way they had come and saw a series of wavy lines marking their progress. They could have been caused by dew, but the grass was dry.

"What, you want a plan?" Butch said, almost smiling.

"To the top of the hill," Norris said, nodding north. "If it's a small island, we'll see all of it from up there. If we're lucky enough to have landed somewhere more substantial-"

"What, like the moon?" Butch quipped.

"--then we'll be able to see where to head for," Norris finished. He ignored Butch, like an adult disregarding a permanently annoying child. Maybe that was why Norris was not really liked; he had no sense of humour.

"Let's stop and rest," Max said. "Have a think about it." They sat in the grass, only fifteen minutes after setting out from the beach. Norris remained slightly apart. Butch picked a blade and slipped it into his mouth, then spat it out with a disgusted grimace.

"I'm so hungry," Max said, verbalising all their thoughts.

Roddy closed his eyes and leant back, supporting himself on outstretched arms. He was aching all over. His flesh felt weak and weighed down by hunger. "We must eat, Max," he said. "Let's leave finding out where we are for later. For now, we've got to eat. And drink."

"Wonder where that tortoise went," Butch said. All four men quickly stood.

They headed across the meadow to where they thought the stream would be, hiding itself beneath the lush covering of trees it had sustained. Where there was water, they figured, there would be food: fruits and berries at the very least.

Roddy felt the silence change from slightly intimidating to threatening, as though they had crossed an invisible boundary. He thought of what Norris had said about the calm before the storm, and looked up into the sky. But the unfaltering blue depressed him, holding no promise of shade from the sun or fresh water to catch in their cupped hands. The thought of the stream made him go weak, because he had seen the dead things in it, and he had drunk the water.

If the island would kill its own, then what of the invaders?

The thought came from nowhere, but it chipped away at his mind as they walked towards the trees. Ernie was already dead, victim of his own knife. But that was an over simplification; the blade had not killed him, it had merely been a tool. Something deeper and darker had been Ernie's undoing. He had been a fair and reasonable officer, but the minute he set foot on the island he had changed. Praising God to high Heaven, but still missing Him, still sensing His absence. Mumbling prayers in the night as if they would bring him closer to God. Or bring God back to him.

God is everywhere, Roddy's parents had impressed upon him. He had believed them because they were his parents; he always did as he was told, and he knew that his elders were wiser than mere children. As he passed through his teens he took on board his own views, and the duty-bound faith he had been given as a child had slowly dwindled, leaving a black hole in his heart where belief should sit. God had, effectively, vanished.

Roddy was often terrified of what He would think if He really did exist. God is everywhere, his parents had said.

Not for Ernie. Not last night. Last night, God had not been here, and Ernie had been abandoned. He was no longer on God's Earth, and Roddy could only hope that he had found his Heaven. Or maybe he was nothing more than a mutilated corpse rotting in the sand.

As the grasses gave way to bushes and trees, and the sound of running water drew them on, the men perked up. Butch came out with a shallow quip, Max snorted, Norris remained mercifully silent. Roddy felt shadows close about him, but they did not bring the cool relief he had been craving. The sun no longer struck his cracked skin, but the heat was just as intense, and pain still bit in from all sides.

"More like a forest than a jungle," Max observed. He was right, though the trees were higher and more closely spaced than in forests back home, their roots visible as if trying to escape the soil. Silence pervaded the scene, a pregnant peace. All four men could feel eyes upon them, and they glanced up into the canopy of leaves and hanging vines every time one leaf whispered to another.

The forest floor was covered with a low, rich green crawling plant, its questing tendrils wrapped around trunks in an endless attempt to climb to the heights. Hints of movement caught Roddy's eye, but every time he turned to see what was causing them, there was only stillness. The light was good, even under the trees.

"I can hear the stream," Butch said, head cocked. "This way. Christ, I'm thirsty enough to drink the Thames."

"Stupid enough, too," Norris muttered.

They headed towards the distant chatter of the stream.

Roddy jumped as something tapped against his ankle. He cursed and staggered several steps to one side, until a tree stopped him.

"What?" Max asked.

Roddy shrugged. "Something in the undergrowth. Don't you see?"

"Probably--" Butch began. But he did not finish.

The ground around them burst apart. Shrill cries accompanied the sudden movement, as the low lying undergrowth parted and shuddered. Whatever they had startled into action scratched at their knees and thighs, then fell back to the ground, scurrying away under the foliage. None of the things were ever still enough to focus upon, so Roddy could only make out a disjointed montage: curved blades catching the sun; domed heads jerking up and down as the creatures moved; feathers floating in the eddying air. Red splotches marking the underside of beaks, like identical spots of wet blood.

He backed against a tree and tried to pull himself up into the branches, but then he shook his head and laughed to quell the racing of his heart. "Birds," he said. "Don't panic."

The others had reacted in their own instinctive ways. Max was kicking out left and right, Butch jumping up and down on the spot, Norris scrabbling around on his hand and knees, trying to regain his lost footing. As Roddy's words registered and the small, gawky birds jumped and fluttered away from the men, the panic eased.

"Scared the living shit out of me!" Butch shouted, laughing with nervousness and relief. Max closed his eyes and shook his head. He looked around, catching Roddy's eye and smirking.

Norris stood and brushed at his filthy clothes. He stretched his neck in unconscious mimicry of the fleeing birds. He did not speak, and when he caught Roddy's eye he turned away in embarrassment. His knees and elbows were dirty and damp from his frantic squirming on the ground. His face was red from the same. Roddy almost felt sorry for him.

"At least we know we're not alone," Butch said,

"though I didn't think much of yours, Max."

"Scared the hell out of me," Max said. He was rubbing beaded sweat from his head, flicking it at the ground. "I didn't realise I was so on edge."

Roddy thought he was lying. He believed that Max was more than aware of the tension squeezing the four men: an anxiousness built up from outside, as well as in, and threatening to snap at any moment. Perhaps the birds startling them had been a good thing, a release valve for the growing pressures of their situation.

"Never seen birds like that before," Butch said. "Like fat chickens."

"Quails," Max said. "At least, I think so. Flightless."

"Why the fuck be a bird and not be able to fly?" Butch asked. His fringe, greasy and lank, hung in his eyes, making him blink. "Like a fish that can't swim." He glanced at Norris, obviously about to come out with some cutting witticism.

Max barged in before Butch could get himself into trouble. "No need to fly, because there are no predators here."

Butch frowned. "That tortoise was a hell of a predator, if you ask me. It was eating Ernie."

"A scavenger," Max explained. He slapped his neck to dislodge a tickling fly, forgetting his sunburn. "Bollocks!" he said grimacing.

Flightless birds, Roddy thought. Mutations. The fittest surviving, a mutation in their species eventually causing them to eschew flight. It all added to the strangeness of the place. "More mutants." Max nodded at him.

"Dinner, all the same," Norris said. For a few brief seconds, the others had not been paying him any attention. Now they all turned to look, just in time to see him fall back to his hands and knees. He scrabbled in the shallow undergrowth, leaves and dirt spinning around him. For a moment, Roddy thought he had lost it, and a terribly bitter idea passed through his mind. He wondered whether the others would have any qualms about leaving a madman behind, if it came to that. He hated the thought, despised himself for thinking it, but an idea once formed could not be destroyed.

Then Norris stood again, cursing some more, and

kicked out at a fleeing bird. Luck, or fate, or something more sinister intervened. Norris's boot connected squarely with the creature's rear end, and launched it on its maiden flight. Straight into a tree.

They all heard the subtle sigh of tiny bones breaking.

"Yeah!" Norris shouted. "Got you! Yeah!" He raised bloody fists above his head.

But the creature was not quite dead. It squirmed at the base of the tree, fluttering useless wings in an attempt to reverse millennia of evolution and regain its flight, lift off and take itself away from its inevitable end. But Norris's heavy boot finished the bird's struggles. Roddy was sure he saw a hint of something dark in Norris's eyes as he ground his foot down.

"I'm not eating that," Butch said. "Roddy said it's a mutant. Could catch anything from it."

Max opened his mouth to explain, but thought better of it. Instead, he headed off between the trees, aiming for the sound of running water. In the distance, calls and rustles marked the route of the fleeing birds. They had still not stopped, as though pursued by something inescapable.

"I mean it," Butch said.

Norris did not appear to know what to do. Roddy stepped past him, frowning, looking down at the dead thing spilling its insides onto the damp forest floor.

"Roddy?" Norris said, and it was the first time Roddy had ever heard the man use his first name. It sounded bitter coming from the cook's mouth.

They left the bird. Norris stepped away hesitantly, perhaps waiting for the others to turn around and change their minds. But Roddy eventually heard footsteps following them, and the dead bird remained where it had fallen.

Bleeding. Steaming. Taking to the air at last.

Roddy caught up with Max and matched his pace. Butch and Norris followed on, muttering profanities at each other.

"More mutants," Roddy said. They walked in silence for a few moments, but Roddy could not bite his tongue. "What's wrong, Max? What's bugging you, mate? I hate seeing you like this."

Max did not answer for a while-- for so long, in fact, that Roddy thought he had not heard. Roddy was about to cover the tracks of his question with some banal remark when Max turned to him; his eyes were dark, and even the sun glinting through the trees failed to imbue them with any real hope.

"The whole world's populated with mutants," he said. "That's the real philosophy behind Darwin. Everyone is different, so simultaneous faith is a foolishness. Ernie was a fool, but he was a real believer, and he was devout. And he loved his faith, and it all came to nothing for him. It fooled him in the end. Drove him to do what he did."

"He was a fool because he believed so much in God?"

"No," Max said. "No. He was a fool because he let his belief rule him. His faith stagnated, didn't allow for progress, something new. It's an arrogance, I suppose, but this place has nothing in common with what he believed in. When we came here, he thought he'd been abandoned. So he used his knife on himself, and gave up without a fight." He rubbed his neck, wincing as the dead skin flaked and opened up bleeding wounds. "That's what's wrong. If faith can't save you, what can?"

"I have faith," Roddy said, but Max looked at him, and Roddy felt foolish.

"Faith in what?"

Roddy did not answer. His words echoed in his mind, as the worst lies always do. As they walked together in silence Roddy realised that, even after all this time, there was something he didn't know about Max. "You've been a sailor all your life," Roddy said. "You've been around. Shit, you're older than my uncle. What do you think? What's your faith?"

Max shook his head, but not in denial. He simply could not answer. It was as though the question of his own dogma had never raised its head. Until here. Until now. A question with no answer, because a man like Max never revealed himself fully to anyone. He was as much a mystery as the complexities he mused upon. A man like Max is wasted in war, Roddy had always thought. He should be creating, not destroying.

They came to a more overgrown portion of the forest.

With moisture dripping from palms and flashes of colour hinting at the secret assignations of birds high in the trees, it looked more like a tropical jungle. The men paused for a while, catching splashes of water on their tongues, listening to the steadily increasing murmur of life around them. Roddy tried to tell himself that it was because the sun was rising higher; the island was coming to life. But he could not help but identify a hidden amusement in the alien banter, a titter here, a low, throaty chuckle there. The animals, now that they had taken the opportunity to examine and test these newcomers, knew the limits of the threat they represented and were laughing at them.

"This way?" Max suggested, pointing along a gentle dip in the land. Nobody had an opinion, so they headed in the direction he had indicated. The sound of the stream was becoming louder, so it seemed that they were moving in the right direction.

They had to pick their way through low thorn bushes, the thorns positively carnivorous in the subdued light. They looked around for something substantial to eat, but could find nothing. Heat was wafting towards them now, as if blown out from some invisible orifice in the island, seeking them through the trees. Their filthy clothes were soon pasted to their bodies, aggravating their already cracked and sore skin.

Each way they turned, they were presented with more difficult obstacles to overcome. They decided to climb the steepening bank of the dip and encountered a slope of sharp, cruelly exposed stone. It resembled slate, but glittered with buried quartz; its keen edges kissed lines of blood into their unprotected skin.

Roddy was certain that they were the first people ever to land here. They must be. The place felt so untainted, so elemental, so pristine. If someone had been here before them, there would be signs of their presence; on the contary, what existed here was a pureness of environment, with no sign of outside influence whatsoever. Roddy had always had a respectful fear of the sea-- nature never intended that man should float in a metal coffin, putting himself at the mercy of the waters-- but here, on the island, he felt even more out of place. He felt that they were four puny survivors of a terrible war succumbing to the dominant party.

What about the shape under the trees? he thought, but dismissed the memory immediately. Shadows. Just shadows. Anything else was simply too terrifying to consider.

They made it up the sharp bank and found themselves elevated, overlooking the stream where it gurgled merrily in a small canyon. The sides were steep, but not unclimbable, and it was only about twenty feet to the bottom.

As he watched Max beginning his descent, Roddy started shaking. Something squirmed in his stomach, scraping at his insides with claws so sharp that he wondered whether he'd swallowed something else along with the water from the jungle leaves. Every step they took, their route was becoming more difficult. Plants sprang out of nowhere, rocks sharpened themselves on their fear, trees melded trunks to form almost impenetrable barriers. Everything conspiring, to make their progress more hazardous.

Yet Roddy felt guided, by an insistent and heavy hand.

He knelt down gently, head swimming, and then he knew that he had been brought here to die, on this small cliff. He would fall and smash his skull on the rocks below, and while Max tried to scoop his brains back into his head, Roddy would look up at the sky, and see a moon he did not recognise slowly appearing against the blue. Like a ghost emerging from the mist, mocking him as his world went dark.

"Roddy!" Max called. The others were already scrambling down the slope, and before his panic had time to take hold, Roddy slipped and slid down to the gulley floor. He did not fall, he did not die, but neither did he feel elated. He sensed the land laughing at him, amusing itself with the mild deceit it had planted in his mind. The stream was the sound of that laughter.

It was gently flowing, cool and fresh, and at its deepest it came up to their chests. It twisted and turned in its little valley, disappearing downstream around a rocky corner curtained by overhanging plants. The men stripped and bathed. There were no dead things here. Perhaps the remains on the beach had been drowned further downstream, to deter any visitors from venturing inland. But here, the air was clear of the taint of decomposition.

The water was fresh. Butch tasted it, then gulped it down. Even Norris smiled and refrained from passing some derisory comment.

"Water, water, everywhere," Max said. Roddy smiled, because he knew what Max meant, and Norris grinned, confident that he'd eventually understand what Max had said. They all drank and swam, and washed away dried blood and caked dirt.

When they had finished, they climbed from the gentle waters to lie on the bank and let the sun dry them. Butch remained in the stream. He bobbed in the current, floating a few feet, standing, doing it again.

The surge came from nowhere. Without even a sigh to announce its appearance, as if air and water conspired to fool the men's senses. Butch turned and stared upstream at the rolling, tumbling, refuse-laden wave of water ploughing towards him. It frothed, like a rabid sea monster angry at the irony of its affliction.

Roddy stood, absurdly conscious of his nakedness. He opened his mouth, but nothing came out. He felt a draining flush of hopelessness, the same feeling he had experienced watching his ship split and sink. No hope, he had thought to himself then, no hope at all for anyone left inside.

Now, he thought the same. Except he whispered it as well, like a prayer to the dying. "No hope."

Just before the water lifted Butch from the stream bed, he glanced at Roddy, and suddenly his eyes were very calm, his expression one of equanimity rather than fear. The look lasted only a split second, the blink of an eye, because then the wave swallowed him in a flurry of limbs. His head broke surface several times, but he could only utter bubbles. The men watched helplessly as Butch was tumbled away from them, mixed in with the wood and weed and dead things also carried along by the surge.

Roddy started running along the bank. Stones snapped at his bare feet. Breath, possessed of sharp edges, caught in his throat. But Butch was firmly in the water's grasp, and it held him close and low, attempting to drown him even before he struck the wall of the gulley further downstream. Roddy tried to shout, but his voice was lost in the angry white-water roar. He sensed the others following him. Their company made it all seem more futile.

Butch could have made it, Roddy thought. He could have swam to shore. But even if that had been possible, it seemed that even the intention to survive had been absent.

In the waters, jumping from the foam which was speckled red for brief instants, Roddy was sure he saw tiny snapping things. They may have been part of the boiling water itself, spinning Butch in its violent grasp. Or they could have been something in the water with Butch, but surviving there, belonging there, revelling in the violence.

Butch was swept under the overhanging trees and plants, just before the stream twisted out of sight. In the instant before he was pummelled by protruding rocks Roddy saw him, eyes closed, mouth wide open. His bruised face had been struck by something, and he was drowning in blood as well as water.

The wave struck the rocks, scouring the blackening surface with its contents, then surged away downstream. It left behind its load, floating in the suddenly calm waters: a tree branch, stripped of bark; a bird of paradise, bobbing like a dead water rainbow; and Butch, his snapped left arm wedged into a crack and holding him there.

His head lolled. He looked like he was falling asleep, and at any moment Roddy expected him to look up and his bashful grin to appear. His head fell lower, however, until his chin rested on his chest. And then they could see the damage to the back of his head, and Roddy knew that he would never be smiling again.

They had to cross the stream to reach him. Roddy could not bring himself to enter the water, even though it was back to its normal appearance, as if the bore had never been. He wanted to mention the snapping things he had seen, but felt foolish; there were no apparent bites on Butch's body, only cuts and scrapes. He watched nervously as Max and Norris waded across, arms held wide for balance.

Max paused in front of Butch. His attention focussed on whatever was beyond the rocky outcrop around which the stream disappeared. He was still for a long time. Roddy was on the verge of splashing out to him, shaking him awake and shouting at him, when he turned.

"No sign of the wave downstream," Max said casually. He looked briefly back upstream, indicating to Roddy the wet, scoured banks where the freak surge had made its mark. Norris seemed not to hear, or understand the implication. He was staring at Butch, disgust stretching his face out of shape.

Roddy was glad he had not gone in. This was not a normal stream, not like the ones in the forests and valleys back home. It was a wrong stream, one which could conjure a wave from nowhere and then suck it back into itself, without having to spread it further along its length. It was flowing at its normal gentle rate once more, carrying away the detritus left behind. The colourful dead bird spun slowly as it headed for the beach.

Roddy thought the wave must be waiting somewhere. Tucked up on the stream bed, pressure building, ready to appear again when the time was right. Like now, while Max and Norris were trying to free Butch's trapped arm without touching the bone protruding through the skin.

But perhaps that would be too easy.

"Get him out," Roddy said, "get him out, now, get him out." He rocked from side to side, wincing at the pain from his gashed feet but enjoying the sensation at the same time. It told him that he was still alive, his brain was connected. He looked down at his pathetic body. His ribs corrugated his skin and his feet bled onto the rocks. His blood was a black splash on the ground. It seeped between stones and was sucked in quickly, the land as desperate for sustenance as they were.

The two men in the water eventually backed across the stream with Butch trailing between them. Norris seemed frantic to keep Butch's head up out of the water, as if a dead man could drown. They reached the bank and Roddy helped them haul the body out. They lay Butch down on the wet rocks. His head was leaking.

Roddy had seen worse sights than this when the ship sank, but now it was different. Just as Ernie's death had hit them badly, the sight of Butch lying cooling in this cruel place felt like a punch to the chest. He had been a survivor, one of only a few left from the ship's crew; he had been valuable. He'd been a friend.

"Just where the hell did that wave come from?" Norris asked. "What caused it? There aren't any clouds, no rain. The stream's back to its normal level. I didn't feel..." He prattled on, but Roddy soon tuned out his voice. He was becoming aware of the expression on Max's face.

The big man looked defeated. His arms hung by his sides, shoulders slumped, water dripping from his ears and nose to splash into rosettes on the rocks around him. Pinkish sweat, coloured with his own blood, dribbled down his forehead and around his ears. The burns and scabs on his head were open to the elements. His eyes looked dead.

"Max?" Roddy said, and Norris shut up. "Max."

Max turned and looked at them, and Roddy saw that some of the drops were tears. The big man was crying. The tears were silent, unforced, trickling salt water into his wounds. "He was only a kid," Max said. "How old was he? How old was Butch?"

Roddy shrugged. "Nineteen?"

Max nodded. "Just a kid."

"Where did that wave come from?" Norris said again, when the others had become silent.

Max looked back down at Butch, shaking his head slowly, hands fisted. "Something very wrong," he said.

"The wave, though," Norris whined.

"Something very wrong with this place." Max turned and went back to where they had dumped their clothes. He hauled on his trousers and shirt, wincing as aches and pains lit up his body. He said no more.

Roddy remembered an occasion several years ago, when he had been more scared than at any time in his life. One of his friends had borrowed his father's motorbike and offered to take Roddy for a ride. Once committed, there was no backing out. At each jerky change of gear, Roddy was sure he was going to be flung off backwards, smashing his head like a coconut on the road. The bike tilted this way and that as his friend negotiated blind corners, hardly slow-ing down. He had the total confidence of the young.

It was not the speed that terrified Roddy, or even the thought of being spilled onto the road. It was the lack of control. The fact that his life was, for those few minutes, totally in the hands of someone else. He'd felt like pissing himself when he'd considered that they were not even particularly close friends. What a way to die.

The fear he felt now was more intense, more all encompassing. It made his terror on the occasion of the motorbike ride pale into insignificance, made it seem like a youthful lark. Now, he feared not only for his body -- a body already ravaged by war and hunger and thirst -- but also for his mind. He was being stalked through the dark avenues of his thoughts, and he had yet to see the pursuer. All the while, the island sat smugly around them. How could logic and self-awareness continue to exist untouched in such a place? A place that seemed eager to kill them, and happy to do so.

Not for the first time, Roddy wished that he had more faith in God. He had seen what belief had done to Ernie, but perhaps Ernie's faith had been too blind, too passive. It was ironic that a war which had seemed to bring many people closer to their faith, by forcing them to challenge their minds and spirits, had driven Roddy further away. While people dying on beach-heads prayed to God, Roddy could not understand how God would put them in that situation in the first place. If He did exist, then He was cruel indeed.

They buried Butch away from the stream, so that any future floods would not wash away the soil covering him and expose his body to the elements. None of the men spoke because they could all feel danger watching them, sitting up in the high branches or raising beady eyes from the stream. It watched them where they toiled, and laughed, and counted off another victory on skeletal fingers.

3. NAMING THE NAMELESS

They headed inland. None of them felt like walking, but they were even less inclined to stay near Butch's grave. The chuckling stream threatened to drive them mad.

They remained within the jungle. It seemed to stretch on forever, as if the grasslands had never existed, and the flora and fauna of the place began to reveal more of itself to them. Much of it was strange. Max seemed to find solace in trying to identify birds and plants, but his comfort was short lived. For every species he knew, there were a dozen he did not. A snake curled its way up a tree trunk, bright yellow, long and very thin. Max went to name it, but then several scrabbling legs came into view around the trunk, propelling the creature's rear end, and Max turned away. Roddy recalled the story of the Garden of Eden: how the snake had been cast to the ground, legless, to slither forever on its belly, eating dust. This creature did not belong to that family. This thing, in this place, did not subscribe to the ancient commandment.

They saw another snake, with gills flaring along its flanks and green slime decorating its scales. Max stared at it, frowning, trying to dredge an impossible name from his memory. Impossible, because the creature had no name. "Slime snake," Max said, naming it.

"You should name it after us, if you must," Norris commented.

"Who'll ever know?" The finality in Max's voice turned Roddy cold, but the big man would not be drawn. He was too keen to continue with what he called his naming of parts, as if the entire island were one massive machine and the slithering, flying and scampering things the well-oiled components.

In a place where the trees thinned out, they saw several giant tortoises picking regally at low foliage. They skirted the clearing, Roddy checking the shells to see whether there was any recent damage. Norris was all for attacking the creatures, but to Roddy it seemed pointless, and Max said something which persuaded them that the tortoises were best left alone: "Why annoy them more?"

The reptiles raised lazy heads as the men passed, watching them with hooded black eyes. One of them may have had bits of Ernie still digesting in its gut, but to the men they all looked the same. Roddy mused that the reverse was probably also true; the idea chilled him to the core, and he did not dwell upon it.

The more Roddy saw, the more he came to acknowledge the alienness of the island. Max's strange naming process only helped to exaggerate the feeling. And Roddy also came to see how they had all had taken so much for granted, and how their ignorant assumptions they had led them into strangeness. They had been washed up on an unknown shore after five days at sea, and at first had put the perceived peculiarity of the place down to the fact that they were somewhere none of them had ever been before. Their sense of disquiet had been heightened by Ernie's sudden suicide, but even that had not alerted them as it should have.

Now, with Butch being snatched away so soon after Ernie's death, Roddy felt like he was waking up. Surfacing from a nightmare into something even more disturbing.

They had all maintained a blind faith in the rightness of things, and now they had been led astray. Just as Ernie's faith had fooled him, so they were being deceived by their ignorance.

"Two-headed spider," Max called out, pointing up into a tree. Roddy gasped and stepped back when he saw the huge, hairy shape hanging there, as big as his head, legs jerking as whatever they grasped struggled in its final death throes. There were indeed two fist-sized protuberances at its front end, though whether they were heads or other organs for more obscure purposes, Roddy could not decide.

"Lizard-bird," Max said.

"Greater-mandibled mantis."

"Three-ended worm."

"Tree sucker."

"Yellow bat."

His naming continued. The men took a chance with a bush of yellow berries, hunger overcoming a sense of caution which Roddy was starting to consider as more and more useless. To protect against the unknown, he thought, was impossible. They were at the island's mercy. And, in a way, this made him more relaxed. He had never before felt resigned to an unseeable fate, not even when the ship was going down; then, he knew he could swim. Here, he was slowly drowning in strangeness, and there was nothing he could do. He knew nothing.

Until he saw the woman. She was naked, her body seemingly tattooed with nightmares, muscles hanging in sepia bunches. She was standing beneath a tree to his left, waving imploringly at the three men. The sun came through the canopy and speckled her with yellow pustules.

"Black lizard," Max called. Norris was with him, further ahead.

The woman held out both hands, her mouth open but silent. Roddy could see that she was shouting. A shadow moved across her body and she seemed to change position. She did not move, but flowed, as she had the night before. She lived within the shadows, as the shadows, and their shifting dictated her own motion.

"Large-headed quail. Big bastard."

Roddy tried to shout. He opened his mouth, but in sympathy with the ghostly form beneath the trees he could say nothing. The woman began to shake her head, waving more frantically. Her body crumpled with helplessness as shadows shifted across the sunbeams breaking through the trees and blotted her from sight.

"Triple-horned toad."

Roddy could not move. He was sure that the shadows had possessed teeth. They had been voracious.

He began to shake and the pressure of the island pressed in from all sides. The ground crushed against his feet, driving them upwards to meet his head where it was being forced down by the hot, damp air. Bushes seemed to march in from all around, the trees stepping close behind, closing in, threatening to crawl into him and make him a fleshy part of them. Rooting and rutting in a vegetative parody of rape.

He thought he cried out, but the only reply was Max naming, and Norris mumbling something unheard.

The world tipped up and Roddy was tumbling, striking his head and limbs, thorns penetrating skin as he fought with the ground. Sight left him, and sound, and then all his other senses fused into one all-encompassing awareness -- that they were intruders, alien cells in a pure body, and that slowly, carefully, they were being hunted and expunged.

Then even thought fled, and blessed darkness took its place.

When he came to, the sun had moved across the sky. The ground was hot beneath him. Norris and Max sat back to back on a fallen tree, chewing on something, looking around between each mouthful like nervous birds.

Roddy lifted himself onto his elbows and tried to shake the remaining dizziness from his head. He felt weak and thirsty, and his stomach rumbled at the tang of freshly picked fruit.

"The sleeper awakes," Norris said, somewhat bitterly. Max turned and glanced at Roddy, then continued his observation of the jungle.

Roddy did not recognise his surroundings, but that meant nothing. This did not appear to be the place where he had collapsed; but viewed from a different perspective, after however much time had passed, it could be, he supposed. Off to his right may have been the place he had seen the woman and the shadows. His skin weeped and smarted with a multitude of thorn pricks, and thorny plants sat smugly all around. Looking up between the treetops he could see darting shapes leaping from branch to branch, sometimes flapping colourful wings, occasionally reaching out with simian grips. Myriad bird calls played the jazz of nature.

He was more lost than he had ever been.

"Max?" he said, but it came out like a death rattle. He coughed, sat up fully and leant forward. The ground between his legs was crawling, shifting, fuzzing in and out of focus. He shook his head again, then realised that he was sitting on an active ants' nest. He shrieked, stood shakily and stumbled to the fallen tree.

Norris glanced nervously at him, then back at their surroundings. Max looked around casually, but Roddy could tell from the way he was sitting -- hunched, tense, puffed up like a toad facing a snake -- that he was concentrating fully on the jungle. Between the two sat a selection of fruits, of all colours imaginable and a few barely dreamed of. Some were wounded and dripping, others whole and succulent.

"Are those safe?" he asked, then realised that he no longer cared. "Not dead yet," Norris said, but Roddy was already crunching into what looked like a cross between an apple and a kiwi fruit. It tasted sour and bland, but the crunchy flesh felt good between his teeth. With each bite, his soft gums left a smear of blood on the open fruit.

"I feel dreadful," he mumbled.

"You've been out for two hours," Max said, not looking around. "You were feverish at first, then jerking and shouting. Couldn't wake you up. Couldn't tell what you were saying, either, but it sounded important. To you, anyway. Had to pull a load of thorns out of your face -- those damn things work their way in like fish hooks. Then you calmed down, after about half an hour, and you've been quiet ever since." There was little emotion in his voice. Hardly any feeling. He bore little resemblance to the old Max, his voice a fading echo of the big man.

"Two hours?" Roddy received no answer. The two men watched the trees, munching half-heartedly on insipid fruit. Roddy followed their gaze, saw only jungle, trees and more jungle. There was an occasional sign of movement as a creature, named or unnamed, skirted the three men, and a steady jewel-drip of water from high in the trees. Nothing else. No moving shadows.

"There was something before I passed out," Roddy said, frowning, taking another bite of fruit. "Shadows, or something."

"What exactly?" Max asked suddenly. He turned, fixing Roddy with his stare. His voice was that of Max again, but Roddy suddenly preferred the monotone of moments before. He wondered what had happened while he was out.

"Well, a woman," Roddy said quietly.

Norris snorted. "Cabin fever." He laughed, but it was a bitter sound.

Max stared at him for so long that Roddy became uncomfortable. "What? Have I turned green? What?"

Max looked back into the jungle. Whatever he expected to see remained elusive; his shoulders slumped and he shook his head. "While you were out, Norris went to look for food. He was back within five minutes with that lot, but he thought he'd been followed."

"Stalked," Norris hissed. "I told you, I was stalked. Like a bird hunted by a fucking cat."

"Followed by what?" Roddy asked. His stomach throbbed, and he felt like puking. His balls tingled, and his chest had tightened to the point of hurting. He realised suddenly how human perception was sometimes so blinkered, so ruled by the present. Until now, they had not actually been threatened by anything dangerous. The island was crawling with weird life, but the only creature that had really harmed them was the tortoise. And even that had been scavenging meat already dead. Now, if what Norris and Max were saying was true, there was something else with them. Following them.

"I don't know what," Norris said. "I didn't actually see it." He threw the remains of a piece of fruit at the ground.

Max did not say anything. Roddy waited for Norris to continue, but he was quiet.

"So?" Roddy said. "What? You heard something following you?"

"No, I didn't. I felt it. I sensed it. I didn't see or hear anything." Norris spoke with a hint of challenge in his voice, as though fully expecting Roddy to mock his claim. But Roddy only nodded, and Norris went back to scanning the jungle.

"Maybe it was your woman," Max said, but Norris snorted again. "We'll have to be careful."

The three men sat and ate, gaining sustenance and fluids from the fruit, not worrying about what it would do to their stomachs.

"How do you feel?" Max asked after a while, and Roddy considered the question. He felt terrible, but he was conscious.

"Must be weak," he said. "From the sea. Maybe the berries were bad. Or the stream water." He felt terrible, true, but also rested. Grateful, in a way, that he had been removed from things, if only for a while.

Roddy watched the trees. He was not looking for the woman because he was certain that he had never seen her. If he had, it was too awful to dwell upon. If she existed, she was walking dead.

There was movement everywhere, and soon he felt tired. "What are we really looking for?" he asked. "I mean...the whole place is alive. It's crawling."

"We'd better get a move on," Max said.

"Where to?" Norris stood and spilled fruit onto the ground, most of it disappearing instantly from sight as if camouflaged or consumed. "Just where are we going, anyway? We've hardly been here twelve hours, and there's only three of us left. It's hopeless. It's hopeless."

As Norris turned away to hide bitter tears, Roddy recalled his own reaction only hours before, when the surge of water had plucked Butch from the world. It was hopeless. He had known, and he had not rushed to help. Perhaps if he had still held hope in his heart then, he would have been able to grab Butch, hold on, drag him from the water's grasp. With hope, Butch may not have had to die. But Roddy could also recall Butch's last glance, and wondered whether he would have welcomed rescue at all.

"Nothing's hopeless," he said, but the words hung light and inconsequential in the air. A shadow of birds fluttered across the sun.

"No," Max said, "Norris has a point. We're walking nowhere. In one place, we can make shelter and gather food. Moving, we're vulnerable. To exhaustion, or to whatever else may be around."

Shadows in the trees, Roddy thought. Stalking. Perhaps even guiding.

"I'd like to get out of this place first, though," Max continued, looking nervously at the permanent twilight beneath the green canopy.

"How about the mountain?" Roddy suggested. "It was our first aim, before we decided to come in here."

"Why did we decide to come in here?" Norris asked. Max did not answer, and Roddy felt afraid to, because he thought maybe they had been steered. Lured by the promise of water or food, but lured all the same. Guided by their own misguided hope, misled by the faith they had in providence. Lied to by the belief they grew up with that, however strange something was, it was God's plan that it should be so.

"I suppose it's part way," Max said.

"Part way where?" Norris was shaking his head, denying the fact that they had control. Or maybe he was dizzy, thought Roddy. Queasy from the fruit. Had the woman in the shadows eaten of it, before her skin was flayed and her muscles clenched in a death-cramp? Or had he seen her because he had eaten the yellow berries?

"Well," Max said, rubbing sweat from his scalp, "from the mountain we can survey the land. Look for help and...well, keep a look out. And it's out of this place, and that's just where I want to be."

"Amen to that," Roddy said. He felt an odd twinge at his choice of words.

"Survival of the fittest," Max said, scooping up some fruit and shoving it into his pockets.

Norris grumbled, "I don't feel very fit."

"A walk will do you good then."

Butch should have said that, Roddy thought. He should be the one having a go at Norris. But Butch was dead.

"This way," Max said pointing. Roddy trusted him. Norris merely followed on behind.

After an hour of walking up a slow incline, the men came abruptly out of the trees, and looked up the gentle slope towards the top of the mountain. On the slope, catching the high sun and reflecting nothing, like a hole in the world, sat the tomb.

Roddy had been eighteen the first time he saw Stonehenge. After the initial shock it had preyed on his mind, its sheer immensity belittling his own existence. He had never been able to come to terms with the time and effort spent on its construction. History sat huddled within and around the stone circle, and in a way it was truly timeless, an immortal artefact of mankind's short life. But it was also a folly: massive and utterly impressive, but a work of affected minds nonetheless.

His shock now was infinitely greater.

The three men stood speechless, looking up at the rock. It sprouted from the ground half a mile away, rising fifty feet into the sky. It was a featureless black obsidian, reflecting little, revealing no discernible surface irregularities. Roughly circular in shape, but rising to a blunt point. Around its girth grasses and a kind of curving, pleasingly aesthetic bramble, bedded in dust and soil blown against its base by aeons of sea breezes, formed a natural skirt. It was a marker of some kind, obviously, and the only thing the ancients usually found worthy of such a grandiose statement was the corpse of a king, or a sleeping god.

It was not the outward appearance of the monument that sent the men into a stunned, contemplative silence. The thing was impressive, but no more so than a warship cutting the sea with the sinking sun throwing it into bloody silhouette. The men's reaction came from the undeniable solidness of the thing, their instant awareness of its existence.The realisation that this place was or had been inhabited, by whatever strange people had built the monument, sent more cracks of doubt through the fragmented image that the men had built up in their own minds.

Roddy despised the island, and he hated this thing. He could see the beauty in it, the sense of history and the dedication contained within its strange geometry. But the idea of meeting the people who had carved or constructed it, the race who could exist here on the island in peace and apparent prosperity, filled him with a dread he had never thought possible. It made him feel sick.

"Oh my God," Norris gasped at last.

"I think not," Max said.

"It's huge," Roddy said. "Massive. I mean, how? It must weigh five hundred tons. It's huge. Massive." He was aware that he was repeating himself, but the words felt right. Huge. Massive.

After spending several minutes standing and staring, the men urged themselves onward. From the jungle behind them a raucous explosion of bird calls erupted, and as Roddy turned a cloud of gaily coloured birds lifted and headed back towards the sea. He wondered whether something had startled them. He thought of the vision he had seen before his collapse. He recalled the woman's shredded skin and bare muscles, the way she had motioned, the wide eyes and frustrated, silent scream.

He hoped they had left all that behind, rid themselves of worry by leaving the jungle. But then he berated himself for entertaining such a foolish thought. The whole island lay beneath them, even though the jungle no longer surrounded them. They still breathed the air above the island, still saw fleeting glimpses of the place's fauna. Much remained hidden, Roddy knew, but whatever haunted them would surely drag itself out of the trees.

It took them a few silent minutes to reach the rock. Max hurried on ahead. Norris walked at Roddy's side, glancing continuously over his shoulder.

"More unusual than it seems," Max said as they arrived. He leant against the stone, dwarfed by its size. His hand was flat and his fingers splayed across its smooth surface, and Roddy expected them to sink in at any moment, absorbed into the sick fleshy reality of whatever it was they were seeing. But nothing happened. Max ran his hand across the rock, palm pressed flat. "Much stranger." His skin made a soft whispering sound as it passed over the surface, audible above the background noise of the island. He took it away, blowing into his open palm and watching the subtle layer of dust cloud into the air.

"How so?" Norris asked. He approached the stone nervously.

Roddy stood back, unable to move nearer, experiencing a peculiarly linear vertigo as he looked up towards the top of the landmark. It felt like he and the stone were growing, expanding into the pointless surroundings, while everything else shrank back to reveal the skeleton of the world underneath. He expected at any time to strike his head on the ground, but his fall seemed to last forever.

"It's so smooth!" Norris gasped, drawing Roddy's attention back to eye level. "Like glass." He swept his hand across the surface, mimicking Max's earlier movements as he blew dust from his fingertips. "This dust is gritty. Sand.

Finer, though."

"Most dust is human skin," Max said. Roddy wondered why the hell he chose to come out with his facts at the most inopportune of moments. Encouraged by Max's comment, he could not help but imagine the rock as a giant altar to some malign deity, sucking to itself the flayed skin of its victims. Their skin petrified and disintegrated, sticking to their god and merging with it, clothing it in eternal, unavoidable worship.

"Yeah, thanks, Max," Norris said. Roddy and Max glanced at each other, eyebrows raised, at the cook's use of the familiar. "That's just the sort of useless fucking comment we fucking need right now. Butch would have come up with something like that, if he hadn't drowned himself."

"What do you mean, drowned himself?" Roddy shouted angrily. His voice sounded muted here, as if tempered, or swallowed, by the huge rock.

Norris did not respond. He kept his hands spread on the rock, leaning there, eventually resting his forehead between them. "Come on. You saw his face."

"Ernie killed himself," Roddy said, "Butch was killed. A world of difference, let me tell you. There's no way--"

"Sorry, sorry, sorry," Norris sighed. He sounded muffled.

"Sorry I said anything," Max said. "Can't help saying what I think."

"The sort of junk that flows into your head, you should just shut up ," Norris said. "Just leave us to it. Just let us get on with things." He stared back down the hill at the jungle, an expectant look in his eyes.

The three men fell silent, each for different reasons, each mulling over his own confused thoughts.

Roddy approached the rock but could not touch it. It seemed distasteful, like a huge living thing, standing there inviting and expecting their attentions. Max walked around its girth, taking a minute to describe a full circuit. Then he did it again, left hand in constant contact with the rock, left foot kicking at the plants growing around its base. Once or twice before he passed out of sight he paused, knelt closer to the ground to examine something in detail. Roddy was curious, but too on edge to ask him what he was looking at. In many ways, he didn't want to know. To some extent, for the first time ever, he agreed with Norris. Max just had the habit of saying the wrong thing.

Or the right thing. And maybe that's why it was so frightening.

"I don't think it's man-made," Max said as he completed his second circuit.

"How do you know?" Roddy was intrigued, even though his heart told him to leave this place as quickly as possible. The rock seemed to focus all his bad thoughts, nurturing them and giving them life. For the past few minutes he had been thinking about Norris's words: You saw his face. Butch, standing in the stream, staring at the wall of water bearing down on him. There had been no time. No hope. Had there?

"Too smooth, for a start," Max said. "It's been here for a long time -- far too long for it to be man-made. It's been scoured smooth by the wind, formed into this peculiar shape by...I don't know. The way the wind blows down from the mountain. Or up from the sea."

"But it's so regular."

Max shrugged. He looked almost embarrassed. "I know. But I'm certain it's natural. There's more. Take a look." He walked some way around the rock, and Roddy followed. They left Norris sitting with his back against its black surface, nervously watching their progress. He kept glancing at the jungle they had just left, Roddy noticed. Waiting for something else to leave it, following them.

Max knelt and pulled back the skirt of grasses and bramble, wincing as thorns pricked at his already bloodied hands. "It dips into the ground," he said. "Curves down. Not like it was planted here, but was always here."

"How long's always?"

Max did not answer. Instead, he stood and glanced over Roddy's shoulder at Norris. From where they stood, Norris was mostly hidden. Only his feet and legs were visible, but there was always the chance that he could still hear. So Max's voice was low.

"There's something else," he said. "Follow me." As he

walked, he talked. "I can't find any tool marks anywhere. Even on what I'm going to show you. It's just a freak of nature, I reckon."

"Like this island," Roddy said.

"This island's no freak," Max replied eventually. "In fact, I think it's pretty pure."

"Pure?"

"Pure nature."

Again, Max had come out with something that sent a cold twinge into Roddy's bones, nudged his imagination into overdrive. You're a good friend, Max, he thought, but I wish you weren't here. Sometimes, ignorance may be better.

"Here," Max said. He pointed.

There was something marring the smooth surface of the rock. At first it looked like a damaged area, where the rock had been struck by a tumbling boulder from above, perhaps, or fragmented by frost over the centuries. But on closer inspection, Roddy saw that this was far from the truth. This small scar on the huge expanse of rock had a purpose to it. A design. Several rows of designs, in fact, running left to right or right to left, each of them strange in the extreme. Roddy reached out and felt the ridged reality of them. He withdrew his hand quickly, because they seemed to move under his touch, communicating their corrupted message through contact as well as sight. There was no sense to be made from them: some were shaped like bastardised letters from an unknowable language while others seemed to have sprouted from the rock, dictated by whatever was inside. They were knotted diagrams, random weatherings. Words from an archaic language, or representations of things too alien to even try to comprehend.

Here, as elsewhere, there was no hint of tools having been used. No scratches, chips or runnels in the rock. If these markings were hand carved, then it was indeed a work of art, though an art as dark and disturbing as any Roddy had ever imagined. If they were naturally formed ... in a way, that was worse. It would be an evocation of Nature's darkest side.

"What the hell is this?" he said. "They're horrible."

"My thoughts exactly," Max whispered. "I really think we should go."

"Are you scared, Max?" Roddy asked. He thought he knew the answer and, if he was right, he did not want to hear it verbalised. Not by Max.

"I've been scared ever since we got here," Max said. "From the moment I stepped onto the beach, I've wanted to leave. And if the boat hadn't been smashed up, I'm certain I'd have gone by now."

"You'd be dead."

Max shrugged. "Tell that to Ernie, or Butch."

"You think Butch let himself drown?"

Max frowned, chewed his lip, fighting with contradictory thoughts. He began to scratch his bald head, peeling scabs to reveal fresh ones beneath. If there was any pain, he seemed not to notice. "I think he had more of a chance than we like to let ourselves believe," he said, finally. Then, as though reading Roddy's mind: "It wasn't hopeless."

A sense of futility seized at Roddy, dragging any hidden hopes he may have had out into the open and butchering them. The black rock stood before him, soaking up his fears, and only reflecting the weird atmosphere of the area. He turned to Max for comfort, but the big man looked as frightened as he felt. More so, if anything. To see a face usually so full of intelligence and good humour reduced to this -- wan, bloodied and empty of hope -- was soul-shattering.

"If Ernie were here, he'd pray to God," Roddy said, and Max nodded.

"I reckon that's why he's not with us."

They left the markings to fulfil whatever purpose they had been created for. Norris asked what they had found, and Max told him that the rock was naturally formed, not man-made as they had first thought. The cook seemed disappointed by this, and Roddy was tempted to show him the markings. To show him that if the rock was not natural, then whatever had made it was far removed from the humans Norris may have hoped for.

They headed on up the mountain. The further they moved away from the rock, the more Roddy felt watched.

And the more he thought about the processes which must have conspired to carve the rock out of the land, the more feeble and insignificant he felt. If it had been formed by nature, then it was never intended for man to see, touch, and muse upon. It was a secret thing nature had done, for its own mysterious purposes. Roddy wondered just what became of those who viewed something never meant to be seen, or touched something intended only to be kissed by the wind and scoured by the dust.

He looked at his fingertips, where grime from the rock markings clung to his sweat. He had left something of himself on the rock, both physically and mentally. Most dust is human skin, he thought. In decades and centuries to come, he wondered how much of the dust coating the monstrous monolith would consist of Butch, or Ernie. Or any of them. And where would their souls be residing? In the hands of God, becalmed and soothed by the promise of salvation and goodness in the life everafter? Or in the rock? Buried in blackness. Trapped forever within sight of life. Teased and tortured by purely human needs.

The island seemed to be changing, becoming even further removed from the outside world. It was as though by discovering this place they had driven it further into itself, allowing greater disassociation from the world at large: a world of people and machines and war, where pride-scars marred every real achievement and genocide was considered fair sport.

Roddy looked up towards the head of the mountain, then back at the receding rock and the jungles beyond. Further down, across the slowly waving heads of trees and through spiralling flocks of birds, the sea stretched out, past the reef and on towards civilisation. A timeless power, pounding itself to pieces on the sharp shores of the island.

The men needed food, water, rest and shelter. They craved all the basics, even while immersed in the extraordinary. There was a sense now, among the three men, that they had to reach the top of the mountain, to see whether there was anything else on the other side. To see, simply, whether there was any hope at all.

But hope too needs feeding.

It died, once and for all, before they even reached the top.

4. NOT QUITE ALONE

The three survivors, hardly talking in an effort to conserve their meagre energy, worked their way up a steep incline. The pinnacle of the mountain still lay above and ahead, perhaps only three hundred feet higher. The slopes here were pierced by dark holes, small in diameter but seemingly very deep. Max threw stones into the first few and listened to the rattle and echo of their descent. He soon stopped, because they could not hear them striking bottom. He said the holes were volcanic, but to Roddy they looked more like throats.

The landscape had changed drastically from the grasslands around the black rock. Instead of bushes and undergrowth, strangely twisted rock formations grew from the ground, with a low, loamy grass coating the intervening spaces. Its blades looked sharp. The rocks were sharp-edged and shone with oily colours, and they seemed to change texture and shade depending upon which angle they were viewed from. Heathers sprouted intermittently, strange, sick-looking plants which gave off a stale stench.

It was late afternoon and the sun was dipping towards the horizon behind the men. They were following their own shadows. Roddy found this agreeable. This way, he would be able to tell when something rushed him from behind.

Norris walked on ahead. He had begun mumbling to himself, his words sounding bitter without managing to make any sense. He glanced around continually, staring past Roddy and Max as though they weren't there, gaze fixed on the pointed black rock receding below and behind them. His eyes were wide, but drained of their defiance; without that familiar expression, he was even more disturbing. And disturbed.

They came to a ravine and stopped for a rest. Max wandered off along the gash in the land, towards where he said he could hear water cascading into the dark depths. He suggested they should have a drink. Roddy agreed, but at the same time he was simply too exhausted to go looking for one. Far better to curl up here, lick the dew from the ground in the morning. Norris simply failed to answer.

The sun was low over the sea, bleeding across the horizon and throwing the ravine into shadow. Roddy sat on a rock shaped vaguely like a pig, facing away from the sunset, watching the dividing line between light and dark creep slowly up the ravine wall. Joan had loved to watch sunsets over the South Wales mountains, he remembered; but at the same time, he realised that the memory of her face escaped him. He had kissed her so much, but when he tried to recall her features, there was nothing there. No voice, no smell, no image of the woman he thought he loved. This lapse scared him, but it was also a comfort. He could not wish Joan here with him; it was bad enough that he was here.

The pending darkness strirred new feelings of disquiet. Roddy supposed that this place was where the beach stream originated, and he imagined the slit in the earth to be inhabited by spiders as big as his head, snakes ready to eat each other to survive. There must be nooks and crannies down there, home to bats, scorpions, insects. There could even be people, strange half-blind albinos who had never even seen the sea and who had only a vague, mythological sense of the world outside the canyon. Next to the rock on which Roddy sat, another rock hunched low in the attitude of a fat-bellied sow. Roddy wondered whether the rocks really had been wild boar, covered by the lava of some ancient volcanic eruption. Or perhaps they too had once been dwellers of the pit, petrified by their sudden exposure to sunlight when they ventured out.

Norris remained standing behind him, still staring back the way they had come. His long shadow had the appearance of a clumsy scarecrow.

When he laughed, that impression vanished. Only a human could laugh like that. Roddy could not remember hearing such a sound for a long time, certainly since before their ship was sunk six days previously. But here, it was twisted into something grim and foreboding, distorted by the ravine into an echoing snigger. Here, it was a laugh mad with something.

Norris was pointing back down the slope towards the

jungle, giggling and sobbing. He backed up, slipped on flat ground and slid slowly over the edge. He cried out as darkness tugged at his legs.

"Max! Max!" Roddy leapt to his feet, then collapsed with leg cramps. As his muscles knotted and writhed he crawled to the drop. His hands left blood smeared across sharpened stones. He was becoming one big wound.

Norris was pawing at a slowly moving slope of scree. He lay at an angle of about thirty degrees, his feet hanging over a sheer drop into impenetrable darkness. No hope, Roddy thought, but he was determined not to believe that, not even now, after everything that had happened. "Best for him if he goes," crossed his mind, and it felt horribly true. Norris suddenly quietened and grinned up at him, and Roddy realised with a sickening certainty that he thought so, too.

The pit was becoming darker by the minute. The sun was not halting its descent simply to watch the unfolding of this pitiful human tragedy. Roddy reached out his hand, lying as near to the drop as he dared and terrified that he too would be dragged over the edge. "Grab my hand!" he shouted, his voice echoing back seconds later. "Grab it, Norris!"

Norris was swimming in scree. For each handful he grabbed, two slipped past him and spun out into nothingness. The fall of the stones into the ravine, a collection of minor collisions with the sides, echoed as a sibilant whisper from the dark. The dark, now approaching from all sides as the sun steamed into the sea.

"Norris!" Roddy shouted, suddenly terrified, petrified that they were all being sucked down, finally, into the island. Butch and Ernie were already there, buried below its misleading surface; now, it wanted the rest of them.

Roddy edged himself forward. Only a few more inches, but enough to grasp one of Norris's flailing hands. The cook's reaction was not what Roddy had expected; he was silent and still for the briefest instant, then he began to shout. The more Roddy pulled, the more Norris squirmed and wriggled, in an apparent effort to dislodge his would-be rescuer's grip.

The pit yawned wide, dark and silent.

Just as he began to slide, Roddy felt a weight land on his legs. Mumbled words accompanied the impact, spat from a red raw throat, rich in blood and confusion. The sound was horrible, the words worse, because they were utterly without hope. Max was sitting astride Roddy's knees, hands curled around Roddy's belt and hauling back with all his might. It was not enough. "He's still slipping!" Roddy said. "Norris, you're still slipping!" Max uttered something between a laugh and a sob. Roddy could not see him, a fact of which he was glad.

"It's so cold," Norris shouted, eyes flickering up into his head to show only the whites. "So cold, so helpless, so hopeless. Where's the point now? Where's the purpose?"

"Pull me up, Max!" Roddy shouted, but the big man was working to his own agenda. He was hauling on Roddy's belt, sobbing, and even in the riot of movement Roddy could feel him shaking. Whether with terror, anguish or elation, Roddy could not tell.

"Oh God," Max began to whisper, his voice curiously louder than before, words carrying the weight of a lifetime. "Oh God, help us, oh God, help us ... for fuck's sake, help us!"

Roddy felt his fingers beginning to stiffen and burn with pain. When he was a boy he had always wondered why people in films let go. He thought them foolish; they knew that to let go was death and still they did so. Certainly their fingers may have begun to hurt, the cramps and pain may have become almost unbearable. But when it was a matter of will -- when they knew that they could either put up with the pain and live, or relinquish their hold and die -- there really should have been no choice.

His grip was slipping. He closed his eyes and gritted his teeth, willing his muscles to hold, cursing them as they ignored his call. Behind him, Max was shaking even more, and his muttered prayers were increasing in volume. He was begging God for mercy, or maybe shouting at him, apportioning blame as he asked forgiveness. But Roddy had learnt enough to know that God would never be shamed into anything.

Norris was still shouting, his words veering in and out

of focus, coherent one second, meaningless gibberish the next. His right hand, until now pawing at loose rock to save himself from the pit, began to push, instantly increasing the pressure on Roddy's grip. He's letting go, Roddy thought. Letting go, in every way he can. What pain is he going through?

"Pull, Max! I can't hold him--"

Everything happened at once. Everything bad. In those few seconds any semblance of control fled into the twilight, and panic took its place.

First, Max screamed. The sound was terrifying. Roddy's scalp tingled and tightened, and a shiver grabbed hold of his limbs and would not let go. He felt Max standing up behind him, letting go of his belt in the process. The big man ran, still screaming, across the broken stones and weirdly twisted heathers of the hillside. Roddy turned his head for a moment, watched as Max ran from light into dark. He passed from day to night with the look of someone who could never return.

Then Roddy began to slip forward across the sharp stones. He was fast approaching what he perceived to be the point of no return.

He saw the ghost. The woman did not appear, as though she had never been there, but made herself apparent. She was floating in the darkness near the centre of the ravine, slightly lower down than Roddy and the still-struggling Norris. She was naked of clothes and flesh, bones glimmering in the failing light, hair sprouting wildly from her patchwork scalp. Her hands were held out, palms up. Her mouth hung open in a forlorn scream, but she uttered no sound. Her eyes were the brightest points in the dark pit, but they gleamed with madness, not intellect.

Norris brought up his right hand, clawed frantically at Roddy's fingers, then slipped free. He raised his hands gleefully, mouth wide open emitting a high, keening laugh as he slid slowly back on the moving scree. With a shout, he disappeared over the edge. His call continued for a long time, and Roddy could not properly discern the point at which it turned into an echo of its former self. Even the echoes had echoes.

From the pit, a smell rose up. Something dead, something unwelcome. A warning, or a gasp, or the glory in a death.

"Where are you now?" Roddy asked hopelessly, expecting no answer.

The world began to spin. His guts churned and he vomited, stomach acids burning into the raw flesh of his fingers where Norris had peeled away strips of skin.

My skin, Roddy thought, down there now, under a dead man's nails. I wonder if he's hit bottom yet.

The woman was still there, but fading, pleading with him to reach out and touch her. But somehow he knew it was a deceit, that she only wanted him to tumble over the edge after Norris, so he pushed himself back until he was cutting his knees and elbows on solid, flat rock. The woman disappeared, hands held out in a warding-off gesture.

He began to shake. The sky was dark, as though the episode had lasted for hours instead of minutes. His limbs jerked and his head began to pound the rock, his nerves pirouetting him into unconsciousness.

To cling to awareness he tried desperately to identify a constellation in the night sky. In some vague way he thought God might send him a sign of comfort, something familiar to hang onto. But it was no use: everything was alien. Even the stars showed no sign of friendship, staring down coldly as Roddy frothed at the mouth and passed out.

When he came to it was dark. The sun had truly set.

Moisture had settled on him, like tiny glimmering insects mistaking him for the ground. His limbs ached, his mouth was dry, his tongue was swollen. His neck felt ready to snap if he moved, but slowly he raised himself up onto one elbow. His back, cut and crispy with dried blood, ripped free of the spiky rocks beneath him. Hauling himself up from a bed of knife blades would have felt much the same.

It was night-time, but he could still see, courtesy of a full, yellowish moon. It hung above the sea, its light shimmering on the surface of the water. Wisps of cloud passed across its face. Stars speckled the rest of the sky. Moonlight played around the edges of the pit, giving it the appearance of a pouting wound, pale and bloodless.

A moderate breeze was drifting across the island, carrying the tang of brine and seaweed, and other less readily identified smells. Decay, perhaps, death and putrescence. But subtle, like perfume for a murderer. The breeze played games with his senses, while his own body sought to confuse him more. He was weak, so weak. His stomach rumbled angrily, calling for food. His gullet felt parched and rough, and the thought of water sent his throat into dry convulsions. Then he noticed that the dew decorating his body seemed thicker than water. He smeared his hand across his torn shirt and bare neck, and it came away sticky with blood. He must have been rolling around, striking himself on the ground, opening himself up so that his jaded blood seeped down between the rocks. Yet again, the island had drawn its fill.

Norris. His shout when he fell had been part scream, part laugh. Roddy had not even been conscious to bear witness to the ceasing of the echoes. And Max had gone too, shouting incoherently, raging and raving into the night even before Norris had fallen. Had he seen the woman? Did the sight of her tortured body, floating in the darkness and gesticulating uselessly, finally drive him to distraction? He'd been shouting for God when he went, and Roddy was not sure whether he even believed in God. But faith was a fickle thing, and Roddy had often seen a sudden resurgence of belief when situations arose to encourage it. Times when simple logic explained nothing.

He felt so weak. In the dark the ground beneath him was even stronger than before, full of power, vibrating with the life it seemed so hell-bent on stealing from them. Perhaps it had begun sucking their energy from the moment they left the boat, finishing with some before others. Now, maybe Roddy was the only one left. Max had gone, and try as he might Roddy could not bring himself to believe in his friend's survival. There were too many holes up here, too many sharp edges to fall victim to.

The sense of being unutterably alone -- not just on the island, but in the whole world -- fell upon him. He cried out with the hopelessness of it all; although he tried to picture the people who must be dying across the globe at that moment in the name of freedom and justice, their plight did not touch him. Instead he mourned his own torpid, deserted soul, pleading for something to fill it, opened his heart up to enlightenment as he had inadvertently offered his flesh to the island. He waited for the light, yearned for the warmth or whisper that would tell him God had found him. Had, in fact, never been away. He recalled his mother's voice as she explained why he should say his prayers every night before bed. "God always knows you're here, but it's best to keep in touch, just in case," she would say. In case of what? In case God was slightly muddled, perhaps, His memory faded by age? Now Roddy thought he understood, but however much he tried he could not bring himself to believe that he had doomed himself simply by not believing. The God he was aware of from other people was not like that. He forgave, He loved everyone. He was everywhere, all the time, guiding fate. But didn't He also steer torpedoes into engine rooms? Urge the cold glint of steel along wrist veins? Blow sudden surges into streams, smashing heads open and laying pagan brains out to view?

But there was nothing here other than the island, and the strange, inbred, mutated things living here. Survival of the fittest, Max had said. Well, perhaps God *had* been here, and found himself severely wanting. Here, something else reigned supreme.

Roddy raged and cursed. He shouted at the dark to keep it, and the things it contained, at bay. His wounds were one big agony, but still managed to create new individual pains for his delectation every time he moved. His agnosticism seemed obvious to him now, but he knew also that he would humbly and willingly admit his mistake if comfort and peace would come to him from the dark.

But the dark gave up nothing. No comforting hand, no whisper of belonging. No animals either. No pig-faced monstrosities crawling from the pit to join their petrified cousins. Nothing.

Roddy suffered his pain and inevitable loss alone.

The night came to life. Sounds came from all around, some

of them blatant, the more frightening ones secretive and covert. For long minutes Roddy sat still, certain that his fear would give him away, as something breathed heavily nearby. He could not move. If he could be as still as the rocks around him, he thought that he might fool whatever was there. Then he slowly came to recognise a pattern in the breathing, and realised that he was hearing the sea, a mile or two away, as it broke onto the reef.

Something sent a shower of stones into the ravine. Claws snickered on rock as whatever it was scrabbled to safety. It trotted away from him, whining and growling.

Then there was a sound which could have been a shout in the distance, or a groan from nearby. Either way, Roddy did not want to sit here and take any more. He was shaking with fear, recalling childhood days exploring woodland hollows and old deserted mills, the feeling of terror slowly taking hold until rational thought gave way to shouting and headlong flight. He could not afford to react that way now, he knew, but still he felt panic and the old childhood fears reared their heads again. Fears of things in the dark with him, things he could not see, reaching out to touch him...

Roddy stood and began walking parallel to the ravine. He headed in the same direction Max had taken, half hoping despite his certainty to the contary, that he would find him sitting on a rock, smiling sheepishly and running his hand across his bald head. Max would come out with some dry witticism, before taking charge of the situation and deciding what to do next. Now that there were only two of them, he would say, they had a better chance. Food, water, shelter for two is much easier to find than for four, or five. And for two who were friends, things were that much easier. So Norris was dead, he would say; so what? So who's going to mourn the death of a Jonah? He would smile as he spoke. Somehow though, Roddy could not imagine these words in his friend's mouth.

Roddy stopped and looked around, vaguely shocked by his train of thought. From the ravine, a sigh rose from darkness into silvery light. He wondered whether it was Norris finally striking bottom. The thought seemed all too possible to disregard totally. The landscape appeared even more alien at night, as luminous creatures threw up flashes of light here and there where they darted or crawled. The mountain seemed much higher than it had before, but suddenly Roddy knew that he had to make it to the top. From there, as Max had said, he would see everything. Whether he really wanted to do so was a moot point. For now it was a purpose.

The dark felt heavy, like the presence of something thick and gelatinous rather than simply the absence of light. His going was hard, pushing through the night, hands heavy on the ends of his arms, feet blocks of rock dangling from his ankles. He was weak, hungry and empty. His mind felt drained, picked over by whatever they had offended by landing here and then discarded, thrown back into his skull like the mess of organs after an autopsy.

The ravine opened up next to him. Dark and deep and cool, inviting, urging him to enter, to forget the hardships of aching muscles and swollen tongue. Another sulphuric sigh floated up, volcanic or organic--neither seemed too difficult to believe.

He thought of Butch and Ernie resting in the ground, the cool earth kissing their skin. He imagined the comfort of lying down, shedding all fears and concerns.

He kept walking.

Each sound moved him closer to the edge. Every screech or growl or cry of feeding animals sapped him some more. His shoulders hung lower, his eyelids dipped shut. Pain merged, physical discomfort and mental anguish metamorphosing into something far more affecting: an agony of the soul, blazing white but invisible in the night. Burning in a vacuum, because Roddy was as drained of faith as any human being had ever been. The worst thing was not his spiritual emptiness; it was the fact that none of what had happened to him had been his choice. He felt mentally raped, but his rage at this was tempered by what he had seen over the past couple of years. The men and women he had watched die. The ships, burning fiercely as flesh melted and merged into their lower decks. The bobbing bodies of drowned men, eyes picked out by fish. Blazing seas of oil. Lands scoured by war, until the virgin rock of the Earth showed through in supplication.

This island had changed him. Now, it intended to destroy him. Roddy was unable to avoid such intent.

Somehow, he survived the night.

There was nothing on top of the mountain. Roddy was not sure exactly what he had been expecting, but the mountain top was bare, swept free of soil and plants by the winds blowing at this altitude.

Roddy was surprised to see day dawn; light was something he had not expected to see ever again. Shocked into alertness, Roddy looked down at himself. He looked worse than he ever had. Blood had dried and patterned his shirt with dark streaks, his hands had been slashed to scabby ribbons, and his knees and stomach had been cut and ripped by the falls he had suffered on his climb during the night.

Below him, further down the mountainside, the great slash of the ravine headed down towards the sea, miles in the distance. The jungle was there, too, a sprawling green border between the mountain and the beach. It looked so alive and lush from up here. So friendly.

Roddy began to cry. If the ravine had been close by he would have gladly stepped into it, revelling in the cool rush of air as he let the island imbibe him. It seemed that the island was holding its breath, and had been doing so from the moment they had landed, yearning for the time when it would once more be free of their taint. Finishing himself now would achieve that end. The view from here was wonderful, the island was raw and beautiful, but it was a vision never intended for the eyes of Man. He was stealing it merely by looking. Even from here, he could see shadows moving beneath the trees at the edge of the jungle, like tigers pacing in a cage.

He wiped tears from his face with the backs of his hands. He wanted to rebel against the terrible power of the island, but he could not muster the necessary emotions. Bitterness manifested itself as desperation; anger brought new tears; defiance ricocheted and struck him as dread. It was hopeless. Perhaps, he mused, it always had been. Maybe they should have listened to Ernie and stayed on the boat. Behind him Ernie, Butch and Norris were already blending into the memory of the landscape.

Roddy stood and turned his back on the way he had come, and walked across the plateau of the mountain top. A steady breeze blew, cooling his bleeding skin. He looked at the bruise on his elbow, the result of his leap from the stricken ship. Now, it was surrounded by other wounds, all of them combining to wear him down, drag him down, ease him eventually earthward.

He remembered another mountain walk. Years ago, in the valleys of Monmouthshire, following in the footsteps of a man called Machen. His parents had pointed out invisible landmarks, but then left Roddy to experience the majesty of the place privately. He had been eleven then, just beginning to find his own mind. Looking back now, he thought maybe that was the last time he truly, wholeheartedly believed in God. Since then, he had seen nightmarish cruelties and acts of sadism. Bravery too, and compassion, but somehow, the bad things weighed heavier on his soul.

As the mountain began to slope down towards the opposite side of the island, Roddy saw the cove. It was at least a mile away, still enveloped by the shadow of the mountain. But the cove and surrounding area were different to the rest of the landscape, marked somehow. Tainted.

In the centre of the bay, obviously foundered, sat a sailing ship. Even from this distance, Roddy could see that it was wrecked.

There was a moment of shock at the realisation that others had been here before them, but it was short-lived. It was obvious from what he could see that no one was alive down there. The area around the cove was dead, like a blank spot on a painting where the colours of life were absent, and sea birds were using the wreck as a roost.

Suddenly, like an animal seeking food, Roddy had a blind purpose. Others could land here. The prospect of rescue did not cross his mind, because he knew he was already lost. But if he did nothing else before the island finished him, he had to leave a message for any future visitors.

A warning.

5. HELL HATH NO LIMITS

Once, Roddy had been part of a cleaning-out crew on a bombed ship. The effects of an explosion in an enclosed space are dreadful, and he thought he would never get over the terrible things he had seen in that tangled mess. In a way, the worst sights were those bodies still recognisable as such. The rest -- the mess on the floors, the splashes across shattered bulkheads -- could have been anything.

This was worse.

What Roddy saw scattered around the small cove sent him into deep shock. The more he saw, the worse he felt, and the more he felt duty-bound to see. Beholding the sights seemed to give them weight, making them real and significant. He wandered from scene to scene, an observer in the most gruesome and perverted museum ever conceived.

The sea sighed onto the beach, much of its awesome power tempered by the reef surrounding the island. The air was heavy with moisture; the sun had yet to touch this part of the world today. If there were any creatures viewing his discovery with him, they were silent. The island was still holding its breath.

They were mostly skeletons. In places, hair and skin were still present, but the flesh had long since shrivelled to nothing or been eaten by scavengers. Teeth hung black and worn from gaping jaws. Orchids grew through a ribcage like twisted, rooted insides. A skull was clamped halfway up a thin tree, face plate split open by the growth of the palm through a void where memory and faith had once been contained. A skeleton lay wrapped around the boles of two trees, hips split asunder by one, spine snapped and bent outwards by the other; the jaws hung open, full of a nettle-like plant, as if the trees still gave it pain. Two bodies lay in each other's arms, half-buried in sand blown by decades of sea breeze. One skull was shattered, the other merely dented and cracked. One bony hand held a pistol. A plant grew from its barrel, pluming smoke frozen forever in time.

Roddy stumbled from one tableau to the next, keening uncontrollably, searching frantically for something on which to blame this atrocity, but finding only evidence of these people's good intentions. A box, lid only slightly askew, contained the faded and pulped pages from dozens of books. Looking closer, Roddy could make out the embossed crosses on their covers.

Rusted knives lay loose between chewed ribs.

A frayed rope hung a corpse from a tree, and a small colourful bird alighted on its bony shoulder. Perhaps it thought the body still held some hidden sustenance, but more likely it was simply gloating.

Unable to look at the bodies any more, unwilling to think upon what these people must have gone through after they set foot on the island, Roddy stared at the ship. It was little more than a rotten wreck, masts long since fallen, sails and ropes torn away by the ageless tides. It was stuck firm, and most of the timber boarding had been stripped from its ribs. The ship, like those who had sailed in her, lay with its innards naked and exposed to the elements. The whole scene was like some sadistic display, laid out for the eternal enjoyment of whatever evil force had perpetrated it.

Roddy had never imagined such pointless devastation or despair. Agony hung in the air as if the travellers had killed themselves only yesterday, rather than decades ago. His presence here felt intrusive. But he was no longer alone.

In the air, he smelled fresh blood and bad flesh.

He saw the body along the beach, but it was not until he stumbled nearer that he recognised Max. The big man was still grasping the rusted, blunted blade he must have plucked from the bony grip of one long since dead. He had hacked at his stomach, sawn the blade back and forth, ripping flesh and skin asunder. His head was thrown back, his mouth open in an endless groan of agony, his bald head caked in sand still damp from sweat. The beach around him was black with his own leaked blood.

"Oh Max," Roddy cried. He felt abandoned and deserted; up until this moment he had still harboured a hope that Max would reappear, however unlikely it seemed. Now, in a perverse way, his wish had been granted. Max was back with him. Roddy wondered which of the strange noises in the night had been Max's agonised scream.

As if the plan had at last been played out, the jungle burst back into life. Birds cackled and laughed, other things cawed and clucked in amusement. Even the sea was louder, for a time. A breeze swept through the trees and set the branches swaying, palm fronds stroking each other with secret whispers. Something lumbered through the undergrowth inland, snapping twigs and stomping bushes. It never revealed itself and the sound of its movement slowly faded away. For the first time since they had landed here, the island sounded as it should.

Roddy felt dismissed.

He reached for the knife. Max's hands still held a dreadful trace of warmth. Roddy grimaced as he parted the dead man's fingers, intending to prise the knife from where it was embedded in muscles and organs and flesh, use it to part his own skin and finally allow his insides the freedom which they so yearned. The rusty handle was sticky with his dead friend's blood.

Max groaned.

Roddy gasped and fell back, feeling nothing but abhorrence for the living dead thing before him. He tried to propel himself backwards, away from Max, but succeeded only in spraying sand into the man's open stomach.

Max groaned again. It sounded as if a cricket were lodged in his throat. His head moved. A muscle spasmed on his forearm, closing his hand tighter around the knife. The movement did not disturb the flies feasting at his open wound.

Roddy was going to scream. He felt it welling inside, clearing his head of whatever rational thought had survived these last couple of days, driving controlled emotions out and allowing blind, instinctive panic to take control. Then he felt himself passing into unconsciousness; his limbs beating at the sand, his head spinning. A black shape stood beneath the trees--the naked woman, her arms held out with hands up, the blackness her clotted blood.

All else faded.

When Roddy came to, Max was truly dead. Several small lizards were clustered around the wound in his gut, darting red heads in and out. They glanced at Roddy between each mouthful, uncaring. He felt too defeated to chase them away.

Somehow, he struggled to his feet. He found it hard to focus, because he had been lying in the sun now that it was peering over the mountain and his forehead was stiff and throbbing. The heat was pumping into his head, boiling his thoughts. The black shape beneath the trees had gone, had changed into something different, something solid. Only another skeleton. This one had been tied to the trunk of a dead tree and the rope still held the bleached remains in place. Weed from the sea had tangled itself around the skeleton's feet. It still had the remnants of long hair, now home to crawling things. Roddy thought it had no arms, so he stumbled closer to see.

It did have arms. Even now, as if caused by some drastic trauma to the bone joints just before death had arrived, the hands remained upright on the fleshless wrists, in a classic warding-off gesture. He recalled the flayed flesh, the torn muscles. One finger still wore a ring, and Roddy thought it may be a treasure.

He had found his woman, his haunter, the shadow that had emerged from the dark to reveal itself to him over the past two days, driving him into unconsciousness. Rescuing him, however briefly, from his surroundings.

She had been trying to warn him, he realised. Trying to warn the others. And then memory flooded back, and Roddy realised what he had brought himself down here to do.

The sea sang invitingly, urging him to enter and fill his lungs. Max lay stretched out on the sand, the knife in his guts coveting fresh warmth to settle into. A rope swung free and easy from the tree branches, complete but for a swinging corpse. Everything implied death, but Roddy had come this far. He was not brave, but he was defiant.

The island could wait another hour for his faithless soul.

There were rusty tools, bleached driftwood, even planks from the shattered ship. The work kept his mind his own, excluding for a while all the intimations of death, all the invitations to do himself the final mischief.

The cross was fine. He thought it would hold.

He tied old rope around each wooden arm and ended it in slip-loops. He stood a thick branch against the upright to stand on and kick away when the time came. The island was silent once more; grudging respect, he liked to think, but he could still sense the satisfied mockery behind the temporary peace. He did not even bury Max; there was little point. The island would have him, wherever his final resting place. He had already bled his life into the ground; now, he was nothing more than rotting flesh.

When Roddy had tightened the loops around his wrists, he prepared to kick away the branch. He thought of offering a prayer up to God, but even if He was there, He surely would not hear anything spoken from this place. Roddy thought that the bastardised symbolism of his own death was prayer enough.

He kicked the branch away and gasped as the rope tightened and pinched his skin. He had heard somewhere that suffocation killed most crucifixion victims. He stared out across the cove, past the ship, hoping that anyone approaching from that direction would see what he had left to them, and take heed.

Behind Roddy, in the trees and on the mountainside, from the ravine beyond the mountain, sounds of merriment filled the air as birds took flight and lizards and small mammals gambolled through the undergrowth. But he felt removed from the island, as if he were already dead, and the noise barely touched him.

As he hung there, he had time to really think about what he had done.

THE END

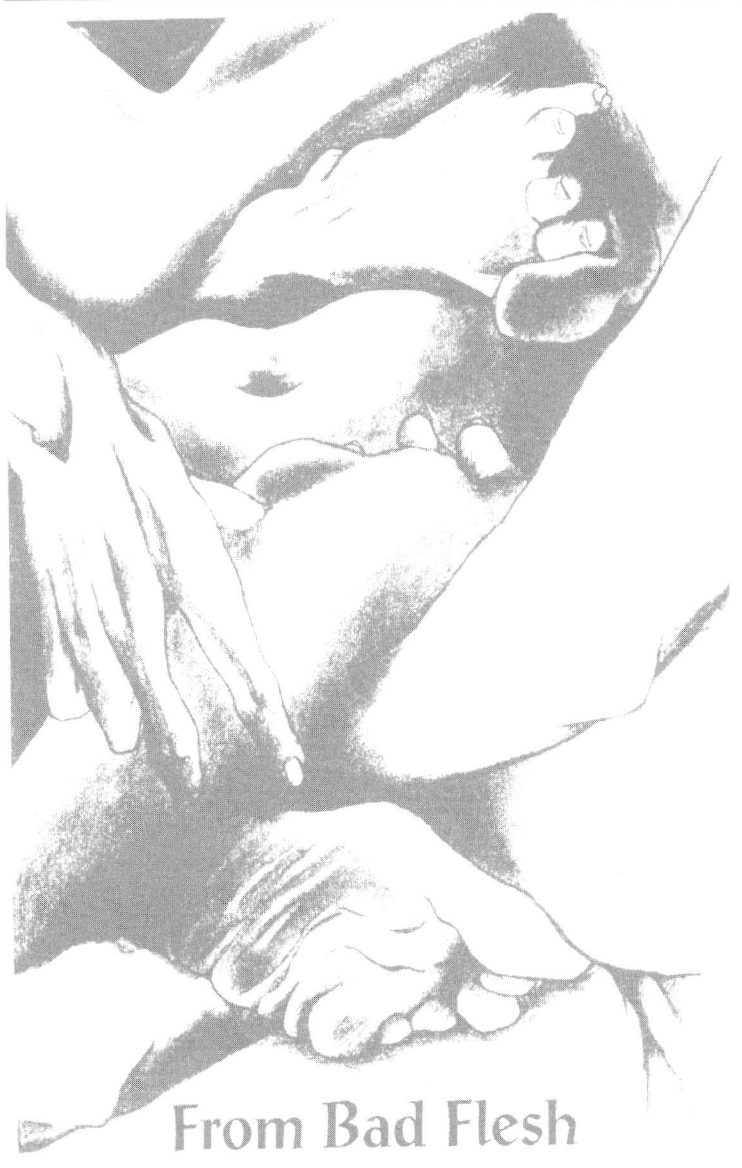
From Bad Flesh

"What's bred in the bone will come out in the flesh."
proverb

PART ONE
BRED IN THE BONE

i

Della is the only person I still listen to. I hear the views of others, weigh the significance of their opinions; but Della is wise, Della is good. Sometimes, I think she's one step removed from everyone else.

She once told me that you can distinguish between truth and lies by the way the speaker tilts their head: slightly to the side, truth; forward, a lie. It doesn't work with everyone, of course. There are professional liars out there who know how to control such noticeable mannerisms; and there are people like Della, who spend their time marking liars. They are the most accomplished deceivers of all. I am sure now that Della has spun me more than a few mild deceits in the time I have known her.

There is a pile of bodies heaped against the harbour wall as I step from the gangway onto the mole. Two or three deep, a hundred metres long. Seagulls dart their heads here and there to lift out moist morsels with their red-tainted beaks. I'd always wondered where that red mark came from, ever since I was a child. Della told me it was tomato sauce from all the chips the gulls used to steal, and I believed her for a while. Then she told me they were natural markings. Now, I know the truth.

"Where do they come from?" I ask the policeman who stands at the bottom of the gangway. He glances over his shoulder at the bodies, as if surprised that I even deigned mention them.

"No worries." He grins through black and missing teeth. "Dead trouble, rioters. Normal, all is normal." He grabs my arm and helps me onto the mole, nodding and never, for one instant, relinquishing eye contact until I tip him.

"Rioters, eh?"

The little man forces a mock expression of disgust, and I actually believe he wants me to smile at his display. "Rioters, wasters, trouble. No more worries." He performs an exaggerated salute, then turns and makes sure my tip is safe in his pocket before helping the passenger behind me down.

I stroll quickly along the dock, sweat already tickling my sides and plastering my wispy hair to my forehead. I try not to look at the pile of corpses, but as I approach the gulls let out a raucous cry and take flight in one frantic cloud. Three young boys run to the corpses and begin levering at them with broom handles, lifting limbs so that they can scour the fingers and wrists of those beneath for signs of jewellery. Evidently they have already been picked clean; by the time I reach the harbour and hurry by with my breath held, the kids have fled, and the gulls are settling once more.

ii

"There's a guy called String," Della said, handing me another bottle of beer and lobbing a log onto the fire. "He may be able to help." So casual. So matter-of-fact. It was as if she were talking about the weather, rather than my fading life.

"String?" The name intrigued me, and repeating it gave me time to think. He'd been all over the news a few months ago, but then I'd thought nothing of it. At the time, I had no need of a cure.

Della stared over at me, the light from the fire casting shadows which hid her expression. Calm, I guessed. Content. That was Della all over. She had short hair, which she cut herself, and her clothes consisted of innumerable lengths of thin coloured cloth, twisted decoratively around her body and giving her the appearance of an old, psychedelic mummy.

She had no legs. They had been ripped off in a road accident, just at the beginning of the Ruin. She was too stubborn to wear prosthetics.

"Lives in Greece. On one of the islands. Can't remember which." She frowned into the fire, but I did not believe her faulty memory for a moment.

"So what could he do? What does he know?"

Della shrugged, sipping her beer. "Just rumours, that's all I've heard."

I almost cried then. I felt the lump in my throat and my

eyes burning and blurring: a mixture of anger and resentment, both at my fellow humans for tearing the world apart, and at Della for her nonchalant approach to my fatal condition.

"I'm pretty fucking far past rumours, now. Look." I lifted my shirt and showed her my chest. The growths were becoming visible, patterns of innocent-looking bumps beneath my skin that spelled death. "Just tell me, Della. I need to know anything."

She looked at my chest with feigned detachment; it was because she hated displays of self-pity rather than because she didn't care. She did care. I knew that.

"His name's String — rumour. He's a witch doctor, of sorts — rumour. Rumour has it he's come up with all kinds of impossible cures. I've not met anyone who's gone to him, but there are lots of stories."

"Like?"

She shrugged, and for the first time I realised what a long shot this was. I was way beyond saving — me and a billion others — but she was giving me this hope to grab onto, clasp to my rotting chest and pray it may give me a cause for the few months left to me.

"A woman with the Sickness eating at her womb. She crawls to him. Five days later, she turns up back home, cured."

"Where was home?"

"London suburbs. Not the healthiest and wealthiest of places since the Ruin, as I'm sure you know. But String, so they say, doesn't distinguish." Della poked the fire angrily with a long stick; I could see she wanted to give this up, but she was the one who'd started it.

"Which island, Della?"

She did not answer me, nor look at me.

"I'll know if you lie."

She smiled. "No you won't." From the tone of her voice I knew she was going to tell me, so I let her take her own time. She looked up at the corrugated iron roof, the rusted nail-holes that let in acidic water, the hungry spread of spiders' webs hanging like festive decorations.

"Malakki," she said. "Malakki Town, on the island of

Malakki. He's got some sort of a commune in the hills. So rumour has it."

"Thanks, Della. You know I've got to go?" I wondered why she had not mentioned it before. Was it because it was a hopeless long shot? Or perhaps she just did not want to lose me? Maybe she relied on me a lot more than she let me think.

She nodded. I left a week later, but I did not see her again after that night. It was as if we'd said goodbye already, and any further communication would have made make it all the more painful.

iii

There is a good chance that I will never return from this trip. The lumps on my chest have opened up and are weeping foul-smelling fluid—the first sign that the end is near. I wear two T-shirts beneath my shirt to soak up the mess.

And if my disease does not kill me, Malakki is always there in the background to complete the job.

The island is awash with a deluge of refugees from the Greek mainland, fleeing the out-of-control rioting that has periodically torn the old country apart since the Ruin. From the harbour I can see the shantytowns covering the hillsides, scatterings of huts and tents and sheets that resemble a rash of boils across the bare slopes. All hint of vegetation has been swept away, stripped by the first few thousand settlers and used for food or fuel for their constant fires. Soil erosion prevents any sort of replanting, if there were those left to consider it. There is a continuous movement of people across the hillsides; from this distance they resemble an intermingling carpet of ants, several lines heading down towards the outskirts of the city.

In the city itself, faceless gangs ebb and flow through the streets, moving aimlessly from one plaza to the next, or sitting at the roadside and begging for food. There are hundreds of people in uniform or regulation dress, most of them carrying firearms, many of them obviously not of standard issue. Whether these are regular members of the army and police force it is impossible to tell, but the relevance is negligible. The fact is, they seem to be keeping some form of radical order; I can see misshapen forms hanging from balconies and streetlamps, heads swollen in the fierce heat, necks squeezed impossibly narrow by the ropes. A seagull lands on one and sets it swaying, as if instilling life into the bloated corpse. Retribution may be harsh, but there seems to be little trouble in the streets. The fight has gone from these people.

I reach the edge of the harbour and look around, trying to find a place to sit. The boat journey has taken eight days, and in my already weakened state the stress on my body has been immense. Inside, I am still fighting; I cannot imagine myself passing away, slipping through the fingers of life like so much sand; I am unable to come to terms with the certainty of my bleeding chest, the knowledge of what is inside me, eating away at my future with thoughtless, soulless tenacity. The Sickness is a result of the Ruin, perhaps the cause of it, but for me it is a personal affront. I hate the fact that my destiny is being eroded by a microscopic horror created by someone else.

Over the course of the journey, I have decided not to sit back and accept it. I wonder whether this is what Della intended — that her vague mention of a rumoured cure would instil within me a final burst of optimism. Something to keep me buoyant as death circles closer and closer. And that is why I am here, chasing a witch doctor in the withering remains of Europe's paradise.

I see a vacant seat, an old bench looking out over the once-luxurious harbour. I make my way through the jostling crowd and sit down, realising only then that this position gives me a perfect view of the long heap of corpses against the wall. I wonder if they are there waiting to be shipped out, perhaps dumped into the sea; I muse upon the twisted morals behind their slaughter, try to remember what explanation the policeman had been trying to impart to me. Trouble, he had said. Poor bastards.

"You ill?"

I had not even noticed the woman sitting beside me

until she spoke. I glare at her. She is the picture of health—at any rate, her health appears to be as good as anyone's can be in today's world. Her face is tanned and smooth, her hair long and naturally curled. As for the rest of her, her robustness sets her apart. She is trim, short, athletic-looking but still curved pleasingly around the hips and chest. Her bright expression, however, is one of arrogance, and I take an immediate dislike to her.

Apart from anything else it is presumptuous of her to assume I even want to talk.

"And is it your business?" I ask.

"Might be."

The significance of the answer eludes me. Thoughts of String are still long term; in the short term, I have to decide what to do now that I have arrived.

My thoughts are interrupted, however, by the sound that has become so familiar over the years. A swarm of angry bees, amplified a million times; a continuous explosion, ripping the air asunder and filling the gaps with fear; pounding, pulsing, throbbing through the air like sentient lightning. A Lord Ship.

Around me, along the mole and in the plaza facing the harbour, people fall to their knees. Those who remain standing, glancing around with a mixture of shock and bewilderment, are effectively identified as people who have come to the island recently.

"What the hell are they doing?" I gasp in disgust.

There are two men huddled at my feet, their eyes cast downwards and their hands clasped in front of their faces in an attitude of prayer. They are mumbling, and I can hear the fear in their voices even over the rumble from the sky. I nudge the nearest with my foot, and he glances up at me.

"What are you doing? Don't you know what they are? Why don't you try to live for yourself?" I say.

The man merely looks at me for a second or two — I'm unsure whether he understands — before remembering what he had been doing. He hits his forehead on the ground, such is his keenness to prostrate himself once more. His voice rises an octave and becomes louder; he is sweating freely, shirt plastered to his back; two ruby drops hit the pavement from his clasped hands where his nails have pierced the skin.

I stare, dumbfounded. "They must be fools! Don't they know?"

"Leave it!" the short woman says.

"What?"

"Leave it! Leave them be! Don't say any more!" She stands next to me and stares into my eyes, and what I see there convinces me that she knows what she is talking about.

Pride, however, makes me try one more time: "But don't they know—?"

She grabs my elbow and begins to lead me through the kneeling crowds. The dirigible has drifted past the edge of the town, pumping out its voiceless message, and now it appears to be heading inland. The hillsides have stilled, the dry ground hidden beneath a carpet of procumbent humanity. I try to resist, but she walks faster, surprising me with her strength. She seems to know where she is going. Within a minute we have scampered into a shaded alleyway and she has dragged me into the shadows, hushing me with a hand over my mouth as I begin to protest.

"Watch," she whispers. "Things can get a bit weird around here."

Like a snapshot of life, the entrance to the alley affords us a framed view of what is happening in the street. As we slump down into the heat, the sound of the airship gradually disappears into the distance. The people begin to rise, eyes cast downward at first; then they glance up, and finally stare forcefully at the sky as movement becomes the prime motive once more. Voices call out, uttering shouts and songs and screams. Some of the people remain subdued, but these seem to bleed away from the streets immediately. Others seem possessed of a frantic activity, which at first is manifested quietly: running, leaping into the air, rolling across the pitted tarmac, bumping into each other, exchanging silent blows. Within seconds, however, their voices have returned; they scream, curse, fight their neighbour, their friend, their family. Less than three minutes after the first people have risen from their subdued pose, the street is a mass of flailing limbs and struggling bodies. It is repulsive.

"You'd better come with me," the woman says. "Maybe you'll be safe if you do. Maybe you won't."

"Makes no real difference," I say, feeling the warm reminder of imminent death in my chest.

"Didn't to me when I came here, either," she says. "Does now. Believe me, you want to live."

The declaration is so unusual as to provoke a stupefied silence from me. I follow the woman further along the alley, soon finding myself creeping through dusty backstreets where old women huddle under black shawls like sleeping bats in doorways. I can smell the mouth-watering aroma of genuine Greek cooking.

As if identity is an afterthought, the woman turns several minutes later. "I'm Jade, by the way."

"Gabe."

From far away, we hear the first sounds of gunfire. The steady roar of the rioting crowd escalates with the effects of fear and fury, and the crackling of rifle fire continues.

"I'm looking for a man called String," I say. We are hurrying through dusty yellow alleyways. Gunfire heralds the death of a few more rioters; my utterance seems melodramatic, to say the least.

"I know, why else would you be here?" Jade does not turn around, but I guess that she senses my surprise. I can almost see the satisfied grin on her face. I bet she grins a lot, at other people's misfortune. Her long hair swings between her shoulderblades as she rushes us through the twisting byways. She seems to know her way; either that, or she has me completely fooled.

Someone jumps into our path, a snarling, scruffy man with Sickness growths around his mouth. Jade stumbles to a halt and I walk into her, grabbing her hips to steady us both. The stranger begins shouting, gesticulating wildly, pointing at the air, at his forehead, almost growling as he motions towards me. Jade shakes her head, very definitely, confidently, and the man shouts again. I can see something in his eye — the glint of madness, the desperation he must feel at the unfairness of things — and smell his degradation in the air: sweat, shit, aromas belonging nowhere near a comfortable, civilised human.

He is mad. He is ruined.

For a couple of seconds, I fear his madness will infect me. Indeed, this seems to be his motive, for he lunges past Jade, hands clawing for my throat.

She punches him in the gut. The movement is smooth and assured. He falls to his knees, gasping for breath and unconsciously adopting the same attitude as the hundreds of people at the harbour minutes before. He leans over until his forehead hits the dusty path, then his whole body shudders as he once again gasps in foul air. A smudge of muck sticks to his sweating forehead as he looks up at us.

"Do we go now?" I ask, but Jade disregards me completely. She whispers to him, indicating me with a derisive nod of her head. In the jumble of conspiratorial words, I hear String mentioned more than once. At each utterance of his name, the grubby man jerks as if given a minor electrical shock. I wonder how a name could have such power; can a mere title induce such a fearful or respectful reaction?

Fear. Respect. From what Della has told me, these are the two things that String must revel in.

Jade looks up at me and smiles her confident smile again. "We can go now."

"What did you say to him?" I ask as we pass the man, still kneeling in the dust, eyes apparently staring at some point a few metres behind my head as I pass him.

"We can go now," Jade repeats, effectively denying me any explanation. I suddenly wonder whether I really want to follow her.

From the harbour — now several hundred yards away, by my reckoning — comes a more sustained burst of rifle and machine-gun fire, and then a stunned silence. Jade seems unconcerned.

I wonder how much higher the pile on the harbour will be by morning.

iv

"In here," Jade says. I follow her through a narrow doorway and we feel our way along a twisting, oppressive tunnel. I hear the scampering of tiny feet, and wonder whether they belong to rats or lizards. When we emerge into a courtyard, I am struck by the sight of beautiful pots of flowers, hanging from every available space on the balconies above us. Then I realise that the flowers are painted onto roughly cut wood, which in turn is nailed to handrails and windowsills. The revelation depresses me enormously.

The buildings rise only three storeys, but they seem to lean in close at the top as if the perspective is all wrong. I look up but can only see a small, uneven rectangle of sunlight filtering down from above.

"Is String here?" I ask.

Jade laughs. "Don't flatter yourself, buddy. Did I say I'd decided to take you to him? Hmm? If I did, I've sure forgotten it." She opens a door in one corner of the courtyard and disappears into shadow. I follow, and watch in embarrassment as she strips off her shirt and splashes her bare chest and shoulders with water from a bowl.

She glances at me, amused. "Surely you've seen a naked woman before."

I cannot help myself. I stare at her breasts and feel a stirring inside which has been absent for so long. She seems to be doing it on purpose, teasing me, but she excites me. She's arrogant, confident, brash, intriguing...invigorating.

Jade turns away and finishes washing as if I'm not there. She starts to unbuckle her trousers, but I have a sudden twinge in my chest and go out into the courtyard to sit down. A few minutes later she reappears, unperturbed by my bashfulness. She is carrying a bottle of wine in one hand.

I have not tasted wine for weeks. The last time was that night at Della's, when she told me about String. The last time I saw her. "Wine," I mutter, unable to keep a hint of awe from my voice.

"Ohh, wine," Jade mimics, taking a swig from the bottle. I feel that we should be using glasses, but such luxuries disappeared during the years of the Ruin. I gladly take the proffered bottle and drink from it myself. I do not bother to wipe the neck. Jade could have TGD, Numb-Skull, QS...anything. But I'm dying anyway. What's another fatal disease to someone like me? It would be like sunburn to an Ebola victim.

"Where are we now?" I ask.

Jade throws me an amused little smile — condescension seems to be her forte — and takes back the bottle. "Globally, we're fucked."

"I meant where are we, here, now. Your place?" I cannot keep the frustration from my voice.

"No, not my place. I don't live anywhere, really. I stayed here for a while when I first came to Malakki, then after..." She trails off, looks away, as if she had almost said something revealing.

"After...?" I prompt. She takes another swig from the bottle and I stare at her new shirt, clinging to her still-damp skin like an affectionate parasite. I think of the growths on my own chest, slowly killing me.

"After I went to String, I was going to say." She stares at me, but I sense that she is really looking at something far away.

It hits me all at once. I realise that ever since Jade led me from the troubled harbour, I have been doing little but complaining and asking questions of a person I do not know. Her avoidance of many of my queries frustrates me, but I did not have to come with her, did I? She offered her help like a latter-day Samaritan — a breed of person that seems to have all but vanished since the Ruin, swallowed into the gullet of mankind's folly — and I willingly accepted. She very probably saved me from a bullet.

With a painful flash of clarity, I imagine my own body on that grotesque heap on the harbour: pale skin splitting under the sun, gases belching out to join the other smells of the dying town, eyes food for birds and rats and street kids. Diseased or not, the dead are all alike.

I have decided to live. This girl might just help me.

"String cured you?"

Jade gently places the bottle on the stone surround of

the lifeless fountain and pops the buttons on her shirt. She slips it from her shoulders and holds it in the crooks of her elbows, her gaze resting calmly on my face.

I stare at her breasts. They are small, pert, the nipples still pink and raised from her recent cold wash. Her skin is pale, but the smoother area between her breasts is paler still, almost white. I feel a twinge in my own diseased chest, then stoop forward to look more closely. All sexual thoughts — teasing my stomach, warming my groin — vanish when I see the scars.

"Do you think I'm attractive?" Jade asks, and there is a note of abandonment in her voice that brings an instant lump to my throat.

"I...yes, I do. But..." I point at her chest, realising the absurdity of the situation for the first time: an attractive woman reveals her breasts to me on a hot afternoon, sweat glistening on the small mounds, and my reaction is to point and gulp my disbelief. But maybe that's what she wants.

"I wasn't a few weeks ago." Jade sighs, lifts her shirt back onto her shoulders and sits on the fountain wall. I see her mouth tense, her face harden, and she reaches for the bottle. But she cannot halt the tears. They are strange, these tears: they clean the grime from her face, but they seem dirty against her skin; her mouth twists into an expression of rage, yet she seems to be laughing between sobs.

I step towards her and hesitantly hold out my hands. It's a long time since I've held a woman, and the gesture makes me feel clumsy. She waves me away and takes another swig of wine, spitting it into the dust when a further spasm of laughter-crying wracks her body.

It takes a few minutes for her to calm down, a time in which I feel more helpless than I have in years. Her rejection of my offer of comfort has hurt me. I feel foolish, upset, pathetic. But I really wanted to help.

"I'm sorry," she says. "I've had a rough few weeks."

"You could have fooled me." I say it quietly but it makes her giggle, and that makes me feel good. After a pause during which a group of old women shuffle through the courtyard, and Jade procures another bottle of wine, I ask the question. "Will you tell me?"

She waves at a fly, wine spilling down the front of her shirt like stale blood. Then she nods. "I've been planning to help you since I saw you on the harbour. It's obvious why you're here. Do you have...growths on your chest?"

I nod. "The Sickness."

"I had it too."

I nod again, glancing at her chest as if I can see the smooth scar through her shirt. "So I guessed."

"And, yes, String cured me." Her American accent has almost vanished. As if she is speaking for everyone.

"He's genuine, then? I'd heard so many stories that I'd begun to think he was a myth. A hope for the new age." I look down at my feet and cringe when a spasm of pain courses through me, as if the Sickness can sense a threat to its incessant spread.

"There is no hope after the Ruin," Jade says, though not bitterly. "Not for mankind. There's personal hope, of course. There always will be as long as there's one person alive on the planet. It's human nature — animal instinct — to assure the survival of the species, no matter what the odds. That's why String does what he does. But mankind was fucked the minute the Ruin set in."

"The crop blight?"

She shakes her head. "Long before that, I reckon. How about the fall of Communism?"

"Why that far back?"

She shrugs. "Just my personal opinion." She looks at the front of my shirt, a hint of concern creeping into her voice. "You need to see him soon, I think."

I look down and see blood seeping through the material, spreading like ink dots on blotting paper. One of the growths has split and started spewing my life out into the heat, and I have the disturbing feeling that our talk of cures and hope has encouraged it. My personification of the Sickness makes it no easier to accept.

"How does he do it?" I ask. It's the question I have been yearning to have answered since the Sickness first struck me.

I see something then, a shadow of an emotion passing across Jade's face. It is only brief, as if a bird has passed across the sun and cast its silhouette down to earth. If I knew her better, I could perhaps discern what that look meant, decipher from her tone of voice what sudden thought had made her blush and twist her hands in her lap.

She tilts her head slightly towards me, and I think of Della. "I don't know," she says. I nod, reach for the wine. Maybe later I can ask her again.

"Will you take me to him?"

"Yes." The answer is abrupt, definite.

"Thank you." I smile and feel a warm glow as my cheer is reflected on her face.

"But first," she says, jumping up, "we eat. Then, we drink some more wine. Then, we sleep."

"Can't we go now?"

She shakes her head, motioning for me to precede her into the building. She slams the door shut behind me and flicks on a light, revealing one large room with bed, fridge, curtained bathroom area and an old computer monitor with a picture of a goldfish glued across its redundant screen.

"Why?"

"It's nearly dark, one." She holds up a finger to count the point. "It's about twenty miles up into the hills, two." Another finger. "People are hungry, three. It's got pretty bad here, lately. Last month they ate two Frenchmen."

I am unsure whether or not she is joking, but the implication of what she has said is so shocking that I cannot bring myself to question it. Instead, I sit on the edge of the bed as she goes about preparing some food. She does so in silence, only occasionally humming some half-remembered tune under her breath. I watch her moving about the room: lithe, confident, her body language echoing her personality. Underneath, I am sure, there is still a lost person.

We eat. Old salad and a sausage shared between us, but I am ravenous and the food tastes gorgeous. I wonder where I am going to sleep.

V

In the dark, memory fails me.

For a whole minute I believe that the hand caressing

my stomach belongs to Della. I cannot bring myself to talk; I fear that this will taint our friendship with jealousy and resentment, but I want it so much, have always wanted it. Della must know that; I cannot lie to her, and even lying by omission seems impossible.

I have never mentioned my love for her.

I know I should turn her away, but it feels so good. Since the Sickness struck two years ago, I have chosen to distance myself from sex; I have to take matters into my own hand. I acted before I was ever turned down, unable to bear the humiliation. I prefer voluntary abstinence to enforced sexual solitude.

I sit up, turn away.

"Oh please," a voice whispers, fighting to be heard through tears which I can just see as floating, glinting diamonds in the dark. "Oh please, don't neglect me. It's been years, so many years. Feel!" A hand grasps my wrist and I remember then where I am, whom I am with. Jade forces my hand to her chest and drags my palm across the smooth scar tissue between her breasts. It is cool, like glass.

"Gone now, it's all gone now." I cannot ally the voice with the feisty, arrogant woman I have known for only several hours. Tears do not suit her. Her beseeching words make me blush in the dark.

"What about me?" Old fears shrink my penis in her hand, sending a flush of heat through my diseased chest. I twist the sheets beneath me, trying to hold back the tears. I feel something touch me, stroke the growths, and I cringe.

"Okay, it's okay," Jade says soothingly. "Wait." She leaves the bed and then there is light. She is standing by the door, hand on the light cord, proud and beautiful in her nakedness. The pale white patch on her chest is almost attractive, set against the light tan she has picked up in the last few weeks. She catches my eye, then looks unselfconsciously down my body, eyes resting on my groin and causing a new stirring there.

"Nobody has loved me for years," she says. She is crying again, but her voice is strong and I wonder whether they are really tears of anguish anymore. She comes back to the bed and sinks her head into my lap; I close my eyes and think of Della, and my overwhelming emotion is a sense of relief that it is Jade here, and not her.

Jade is wild. Our lovemaking is fast and furious, passion-filled and almost violent in its intensity. By the end we are both crying. She remains sitting astride me, wiping tears from my cheeks, and I kiss her salty eyes and whisper that she is beautiful.

"How could you, when...?" I ask, half-pointing to my chest with unwilling fingers.

"You'll be beautiful too, soon," she says. Nobody has ever called me beautiful before. I like it.

In the morning we wake late. Passion seems to have fled with the dark, and although we smile and kiss it feels more as friends.

vi

"String is in the hills." Jade is tightening the straps on her rucksack, checking the lid is screwed onto her water bottle, rubbing sun cream onto her bare legs and arms. She hands me the bottle and I smear my balding scalp with cream.

"How will we get there? Last night you said twenty miles; that's a long way to walk. I'm not so strong, lately."

"Maybe we can hitch a ride with a Lord Ship," she smiles. "Come on."

It is even hotter than the previous day, and before long sweat has pasted my shirt to my sickly body and soaked through to darken the material. I can feel the sun working on my arms and trying to find a way through the cream, and I guess that I'll end up getting horribly burnt whatever measures I take to prevent it.

Jade has changed. She's still the no-nonsense girl I met the previous day, but she seems somehow more relaxed in my company. There is still an undefined tension, however, a distance that I cannot help but feels sad at.

After last night, I would have hoped for more.

PART TWO
THE TRAPPINGS OF THE FLESH

i

"Faith is as personal and as private as a thing can be," Della once told me. "If you understand someone's faith, you know their soul. But most people aren't very comfortable with the idea of personal faith. Sometimes, it's just too much effort, too challenging. They have to ascribe to some pre ordained vision of things, where there are books and preachers and teachers to lead them through the minefield of knowledge. Prophesies tell them what they need to know, words written millennia ago by some holy man drunk on monastery wine and eager to bury his cock in the young girl from the local village. Then, they wonder why their faith lets them down so much, and causes wars and death and hatred. Simple reason — it's not their faith. It's a ready-made idea of faith. Dehumanised — just add belief."

It was a hot summer's day, only a couple of years before the Ruin really took hold and threw people back two hundred years into anarchy and poverty. Della sat in a garden chair, reaching over every now and then to snatch a sweet from the table next to her. I was lying on the lawn, mindful of insects and ants, feeling the sun cook my exposed scalp but not really caring. The sunburn would be a brand of the day, a reminder of what Della was telling me. She was a wise woman; I knew nothing. I loved her.

"Have you faith?" she asked.

The question surprised me, but I felt I recovered well "Of course."

"Good." She said no more. I was afraid that she would ask me what my faith rested on; she'd know if I lied, she'd read me like a large-print book held under a magnifying glass. Because, in truth, my faith was based solely on her. I wonder whether she ever really knew that.

"You may need it one day."

She did not look at me. She stared into the eye-blue sky, a strange smile on her face. A smile I did not like. She carefully took another sweet from the table without looking at what she was doing; she could just as easily have snatched up a bug to eat.

"Why?" I said, finally.

She glanced down at me, then nodded up at the sky as if the fluffy white clouds could explain everything. "Bad days coming."

Fuck, was she right.

ii

Jade leads me through the warren of alleys and side streets until we emerge onto a main thoroughfare. The rucksack already feels heavy against my shoulders, pressing against my back and causing my shirt to slip back and forth across my damp skin. The cream I had applied is already redundant, and I feel as though my skull is getting ready to tear through the skin on my head. There's no real protection anymore other than staying out of the sun altogether, but skin cancer is the least of my concerns.

The streets are surprisingly quiet; the few groups of people there are seem to be milling aimlessly rather than actually going places. I see several people who are obviously not Greek; none of them appears sane. They scrabble in the dust for dog-ends, fighting over a few flakes of rough tobacco. Growths have turned their bodies into grotesque parodies of people, walking warts that gibber and leak from various orifices. I catch up with Jade and walk by her side, her presence giving me a comfortable sense of safety. She's seen all this before; she knows what to expect; she can handle herself.

I wonder whether these people came to be cured.

"They're all wasters," Jade says in answer to my thoughts. The expression reminds me of the uniformed man who helped me from the boat, the way he had spoken of the piled corpses. "Some of them were given the opportunity, apparently, but they wasted it. Now, they're down to this. They even worship the Lord Ships." She seems to have slipped into her own private conversation, excluding me completely. "Strange how we regress so easily."

"But they must know about the Lord Ships?" I say, confusion twisting my voice into a whine.

"Hmm?" Jade looks at me as if she'd forgotten I was there, and a brief pang of resentment stabs at my chest. She wasn't like this last night; not when she was riding me, sweating her lust over me. "Oh, yeah, they know," she says. "That's what I mean. They know the Lord Ships are unmanned, automatons, pilots dead or gone. But they've been here for a while, and I suppose in their state the fears of the locals drive their certainties back out."

We pass a group of young men and women who regard us with a mixture of anger and fear. I can understand why they would be angry with us— aliens in their country, invaders in a world shrinking back to almost tribal roots — but what do they fear?

"Why don't the locals know about the Lord Ships?" I ask.

"Oh, they do. They just choose not to believe it."

I can scarcely credit this myself; the fact that a civilised people can let themselves be controlled by ghosts from the past, willingly prostrating themselves at the feet of dead gods, knowing all the time that their actions are a sham. I ask Jade why this is so. I do not like the answer I receive.

"God is dead," she says. "That's what anyone here will tell you if you ask them. Do you know what these people have been through since the Ruin? Their population was halved by CJD-2; the Turks decided to nuke the north of the island for the hell of it; and, at the end, when it all went totally fucking haywire, the Lord Ships condemned them as heathens and witches. Sentenced them to death. It was only the fall of the Lord Ships that saved them."

"And now they worship them all the more since they're dead and gone?"

"As I said," Jade confirmed with a sardonic smile, "God is dead. He let them be dragged through hell, now they hate Him for it."

"Do you believe He's still there?" I ask. I surprise myself with my frankness about a subject I feel so confused and cynical about. I have never believed in God; I have my own faith.

"I have my own faith," Jade says quietly.

I think of Della, smile, wonder where she is now, what she's doing. Sitting back and sharing her infinite wisdom with some other sucker, no doubt. A pang of jealousy tickles my insides, but I force it out and tell myself that Della would hate me for it.

"Here we are." Jade has stopped in front of what was obviously once an affluent hotel. Now it seems to exclusively house prostitutes between the ages of fifteen and fifty. A dozen of them sit in broken chairs on the cracked patio and they appraise me, laughing and jeering, as I step behind Jade. My face colours, but I secretly enjoy the attention. Last night has kick-started my libido.

Jade talks to the women in Greek and waves profuse thanks as she backs away from the hotel. I back away with her, wondering whether it's a ritual of sorts or simple politeness, but the women are laughing again. A dog runs by and nearly trips me up; it's a mangy mutt, but seems well fed. I remember the pile of corpses along the harbour and wonder what it's been feeding on, and my sense of humour quickly flees. The women seem to sense this and stop laughing.

"Follow me," Jade says, somewhat impatiently.

"Where?"

"Bikes." She strides around the corner of the hotel.

In what used to be the swimming pool there are at least a hundred bicycles of all shapes and sizes, ranging from a rusty kiddie's tricycle to a three-wheeled, panniered stainless steel monster that would have set me back a month's salary in the days before the Ruin. I wonder what the owner would want for it now. The bikes fill the pool, a tatty metallic pond of tortured frames, tired tyres and accusing spokes. Dust has blown down from the depleted hillsides and formed drifts at the edges of the pool, like frozen waves trying to reclaim it. I see the remains of what I'm sure is a dead dog, buried beneath the network of wheels, handles and pedals. I try to imagine its panic as it realised that the strange, surreal landscape it had slunk into had effectively trapped it. It must have been cooked to death by the relentless sun.

"You Yankee?" says a huge man sitting under an awning.

"No, English," Jade replies instantly. I've already been here long enough to know that there must be a reason for her denying her nationality.

"Good. Hate Yankee. Fuckin' killing bastards, Yankees."

Jade nods and smiles, and this seems to secure her the big man's favour. "We'd like a couple of bikes, if you have any to spare," she says, unfazed by his vitriol.

He laughs, a sound that would have seemed ridiculously overblown had it not been for the machine pistol dangling from his belt. As he bellows his mirth at the sky, I take the opportunity to size him up. He's not just big, he's massive, at least twenty-five stone of flesh, all of it sweaty and sickly and grey. He's wearing a pair of Bermuda shorts which are grotesquely too small for him, cutting into his flesh and stretching out in places like the skin on overcooked sausages. With each shudder of his body, I fear they will burst. His bare chest is studded with black, oozing growths. I'm amazed at how hearty he seems.

"You want bikes? I find you one or two." He waves his hand at the pool, as if drawing our attention to a fine display of quality antiques. In a way, I think to myself, they are. "But the final question as always, lady: price?"

"I've got your price," she says, heaving her rucksack from her shoulders. Her loose shirt flaps open and I catch a glimpse of her breasts swinging freely as she bends down; I suddenly fear what this fat man's price will be, and wonder how close I would get before he could unclip the gun from his belt.

"I'll take the shiny trike and the hefty mountain bike," Jade says, pulling a small package from the backpack.

"Hmm, big spending if you want those, little lady," Fat Man says. I hear something I don't like in his voice — it is quieter, more serious — and I tense as he stretches his neck in an effort to see down Jade's top. The Sickness picks a bad time to announce its presence to me, jabbing at my chest with white-hot fingertips of pain. I groan and swoon, but pinch a twist of skin on my leg to prevent myself from fainting.

Jade glances back at me and moves off towards Fat Man. She whispers something to him, actually standing on tiptoe so that she can speak into his ear, one hand resting on his pendulous stomach. I can barely imagine how she could give him a better chance to grab at her, but he does not. Instead, his grim expression is transformed into one so child-like and angelic that I almost laugh out loud.

Jade turns, looks at me, nods towards the pool of bikes. I wonder what the hell she has told him. I sidle sideways and lean across the heap of metal, grabbing the handlebars of the stainless steel trike and tugging hard.

Within minutes we are away, the Fat Man calling cheerfully after us, telling us to watch out for the fuckin' murdering Yankees.

Jade takes the mountain bike, I'm on the trike. I'm surprised to find it well-oiled and maintained, the brakes old but well-adjusted, the saddle soft and pliable.

"Two questions," I start, but both are obvious. She eases back until she is pedalling alongside me; we are travelling two abreast along the main road, but there is no motor traffic.

"He hates Americans because the rest of the world does," she says. "We're blamed for it all. The wars. The starvation. The Ruin." She's silent for a moment, and I'm about to ask my second question when she continues. "He should visit the States sometime, see what's left of it." She pedals harder and slips down a gear, motoring on ahead. Her move offers me a pleasing view of her rump, flexing as her legs pump her along the degenerating tarmac.

"Second question," she says, "is what did I give him? Right?" She glances back over her shoulder and I nod. "None of your fucking business." I try to hear a joke in her voice, but there is none. Or if there is, she's hiding it well.

We pedal for an hour in silence, Jade leading, me following comfortably on the trike. More than once I think of asking her whether she wants to swap, but my body is stiffening and burning as the infected blood from the growths on my chest surges once more into my veins. One day, a surge like this will kill me. One day soon — perhaps today, riding this bike, my feet describing thousand of circles an hour — black blood will leak from a growth and block an artery, popping a dozen blood vessels at a time until I die. If I'm lucky, it may only take a minute or two.

On the outskirts of the town we pass through the ribbon of huts and tents which makes up the camp of the homeless. Eyes follow us on our way, but there is little real interest there. Even the children I see appear old, apathetic and grim instead of lively and playful. We pass a body at the side of the road. A sick fascination forces me to slow down so that I can properly see the dog chewing at its open stomach. There are lizards here, too, darting in and out of the empty eye-sockets to dine on the delicate morsels within.

We pass by. Jade seems unconcerned, but I cannot help but stare out over the sea of torn tents and makeshift hovels. There are families of eight living in one tent; great open ditches full of shit and flies and the discarded bodies of the dead; queues to full buckets at a meagre stream, the liquid resembling diseased effluent rather than water. Smells assault me physically, the stench clutching my stomach and throat in its acidic grip. But throughout the ten minutes it takes us to pass through the shantytown, Jade does not slow down once. She does not glance to either side. She does not seem to care.

But she has seen it all before.

As we leave Malakki Town and head into the surrounding hills, there is a change. I can feel it in the air, a potential that I cannot describe or adequately read. Jade senses it too; she keeps glancing back at me as if afraid I have begun to lag behind. In truth, I feel as energized and excited as I have for months, a power pumping through my muscles which has more to do with my sense of freedom than the potential cure I am travelling towards.

The new aura of well-being makes me think about the night before: the passion we had for each other, as if love were at a dirth.

There is a gunshot. Jade's bike swerves, then leaves the road, flipping over into the dry ditch. I hear a scream, and for a terrible few seconds I cannot tell whether it is Jade's voice, or my own. Then, more gunshots, breaking the air apart like the answer to a prying question.

iii

The hillside is smooth, stripped bare of plant life, topsoil scoured away by the biting winds; sound travels further here. The gunfire — sustained, explosive — is coming from around a bend in the road ahead. The perpetrators, and the executed, are hidden from sight by an old stone wall.

Jade curses bitterly, trying to untangle her legs from the wreckage of the bicycle. I notice that she is keeping her head down almost without thinking about it, and I wonder how many shoot-outs she's witnessed. I crawl along the dry ditch, leaving the trike behind me, hands reaching out to drag the bike back from her legs. I try to tell her to keep still, but the gunfire has increased to a screaming crescendo and she can only frown at my words.

Eventually, through a combination of her kicking and me pulling, she extracts her legs from the twisted bike. There is a raw gravel burn on her left leg; blood is already seeping from a hundred pinpricks in the skin and merging into angry red rivulets. She sucks her palm, spitting out black pellets of stone, sucking again, spitting again. I feel queasy watching her, and then the Sickness chooses this most inopportune of moments to send me into a faint.

The gunshots fade away — either the shooting has finished, or I'm really losing it. I slump in the ditch, Jade staring at me past the splayed fingers of her right hand, palm pressed to her mouth. The last image I see is Jade, spitting a mouthful of blood and gravel into the air, and the sun hiding behind clouds like the ghost of an airship.

iv

"About time," the voice says.

I open my eyes and grimace as the sun dazzles me. I feel heat on my front, and realise instantly that my shirt has been removed. The sun is slowly cooking the growths on my chest, turning them an angry red as if they are embarrassed at their nakedness.

"How long...?" is all I can manage.

"Half an hour," Jade says, leaning into view. She tips a water bottle over my face and then splashes more across my body. I flinch, but then sigh with pleasure.

Groggily, I sit up. I realise that the hillside is silent, just as I see the crimson mess of Jade's hand holding the bottle. "Oh Christ, your hand." I reach out, but she withdraws.

"It's all right! Bloody, that's all, looks worse than it is."

She has washed her leg and is wearing what look like her knickers as an improvised bandage. She looks away from me, as if ashamed of her wounds, and wraps a strip of cloth from her shirt around her hand. It is instantly soaked red. She cringes, flexes her hands and draws an uncomfortable breath.

"How you feeling?" she asks.

Memory suddenly jerks me upright, instils me with a sense of urgency. "Where are the guns? Who was shooting?"

"Don't worry, while you were doing your Rip Van Winkle they got into a truck and drove off."

"Did they see us?"

"If they had you wouldn't have woken up."

I try to stand, sway, sit down again. "Who were they shooting at?"

Jade looks up the gentle hillside, trying to see past the crumbling wall. "Well, I reckon that once we get moving again, we'll find out."

"So many guns..." I say, trailing off and leaving the obvious unsaid. So many guns, how many people?

We haul the tricycle from the ditch, brushing off the accumulated rubbish of decades. Apart from a twisted spoke or two the machine is undamaged, but that's more than can be said for Jade's bike. It is a ruin, all pointing spokes and bent frame, the saddle deformed almost ninety degrees out of true. The front wheel is buckled beyond repair; the rear tyre is flat and shredded. I realise how lucky Jade has been; she has a torn hand and slashed leg, true, but if the ground had been as unkind to her as it was to her bike, we'd be looking at more than a bit of leaking blood right now.

"You were lucky," I say.

She nods. "Come on, we'd better get a move on."

"Jade."

"What?"

"Why are you so pissed with me?"

She stares at me. I realise how old she looks behind the superficial attractiveness, how her eyes never really laugh but bear whatever terrible things she has seen like a brand. I wonder how I would feel if I were cured of the Sickness; I like to think it would give me a new-found energy, a reason to be grateful, a duty to thank life every single day. I know Della would want that; I put my faith in Della, I always have.

"I'm not pissed at you, Gabe. Oh Christ, it's something you'll understand soon enough."

Her words scare me more than I'd like to admit, burrow their way into my thoughts like insubstantial maggots. "What are you leading me to?" I ask, for the first time. Until now, I'd trusted her implicitly. A stupid reaction to someone I didn't know, maybe, but there really had been no reason to think otherwise. And she seemed to know what she was doing, she was streetwise and confident, she knew things like how to get the bikes and how to get me to String. But just what the hell had I really gotten myself into?

"I'm leading you to a man called String. He's a bit of a witch doctor, I suppose you'd say." She punctuated each point with a nod of the head, as if explaining to me the rules of a game instead of the particulars of our current, worrying situation. "String can cure people of the Sickness — he cured me," she continues, tapping her chest. "But on the way to where String is, you're likely to see some nasty things. That's just the nature of things — the way things have to be. It doesn't really matter, sometimes it's just got to happen. But the things you see might not be nice. Like what's around that corner."

She waves a hand over her head, then turns and gazes in the direction she had indicated, giving me her back to stare at as she continues. "I've been this way once before, remember. I've seen these things already; I've experienced them. The Ruin's a right fucker, but just when you think you've seen everything bad it's got to throw at you, there's something else. But some bad things are good as well." She turns back, and her haunted expression sends a shiver down my spine. "Remember that. There are sayings: Cruel to be kind. Good comes from evil." She bends and sighs as she eases her rucksack onto her shoulders. "I'm not pissed at you. I'm just not looking forward to seeing all the bad stuff again."

"What bad stuff?" Her words have planted the fear of damnation in me, sent an arrow of terror streaking through my veins and pincering my heart between its dozens of heads. "What am I going to see?"

Jade nods at the tricycle, indicating that I should travel on it, then walks on ahead. "Best see for yourself. Up here. Around the corner."

At first I think it's a stagnant pond. There is a light steam rising from it, though the surface appears uneven and is scattered with protruding growths of fungi. Then I realise what I am really seeing. In a dip in the ground — perhaps where water had once gathered naturally, before the Ruin decimated the atmosphere of the planet — there is a lake of twitching bodies. The movement I had mistaken as ripples on the surface of the water is their dying shiver, transferred through the hundreds of corpses like an electric shock. There *is* a pool, of sorts: the bodies lay in a quagmire of blackened, soupy mud, dust having sucked up their spilled blood and spread underneath them. The steam is rising from this, like nebulous spirits making their final journey.

But surely there can be no peace here. Not here, where for every five bodies that lie still there is one still alive, squirming silently in the white-hot agony of approaching death. Not here, where the stark white eye of a dead child stares from an otherwise shattered face. No peace here, where the rich stench of death and dying is a meaty tang in the hot air.

I stop pedalling and the trike drifts to a tired pause in the middle of the road. I cannot begin to estimate the number of bodies; the shock has frozen my mind, the sheer unexpectedness of this sight paralysing my thoughts.

In the city, yes, I had seen the great mound of corpses along the quay. But there, perversely, it had not seemed obtrusive. Maybe it was the casual way that people had regarded the bodies, barely looking at them, treating them more as a landmark than an object of pity or disgust. In the city, I had been prepared for anything. The Ruin has changed so much, and the face of humanity has changed with it, seemingly regressing to ages past.

But here...in the country...on a hillside that had once been beautiful, and could be again, the sight is almost surreal in its contradictions: the deep blue of the sky, decorated with an occasional cloud cheerful in its fluffiness; and the bloody red mess of open meat, steaming insides, pulsing wounds...

I begin to cry. I cannot help myself and Jade, in her defence, moves away and sits under a tree stripped of life years ago. The tears are hot and heavy in the furnace of approaching midday, streaking the dust on my face and falling onto my shirt, where they merge with sweat and the leakings from my growths to form a liquid testament to my wretchedness.

I sit that way for several minutes, willing the tears to stay because they blur my vision and camouflage the sight before me. Then Jade walks over to me and places a hand on my shoulder.

"I don't understand," I say, realising the stupidity of the statement. Who could possibly claim to understand the insanity of this moment?

But Jade seems to.

"There are lots of reasons," she says. "Population control, for one. At least half of those you see are children. The others are men and women of a ...breeding age. No old people. No ill people."

"But that's just...so misguided. So wrong. How can anyone think this can help?"

Jade is silent for a moment. She seems to be staring over the bodies, perhaps glimpsing some vague future that lies beyond their steaming deaths, but nearer than we think.

"But it does work," she says, pained. "More food, more medicine, more water. Times have changed, you know, since the Ruin."

"I never dreamed..." I cannot finish. I can barely comprehend the terrible truth of what I have seen. On the harbour, the bodies...I suppose I thought that they had died in some natural, acceptable way, and had been merely stored or placed there. The gunshots I heard, the shouts, the riots...I had placed these in a mental file marked 'Disregard'. Even with my own tenuous hold on reality, perverted by the Ruin, I could never stoop so low as this, and so my mind precluded the possibilities laid out so obviously for me to see.

"I don't believe it," I say. I have stopped crying, but the anguish is even deeper now that the tears have dried. "It's just horrible."

"I'm sorry," Jade says suddenly, "I should have warned you. But I..."

I smile up at her where she stands next to the tricycle, reach for her uninjured hand and feel a warm rush of relief when she returns the pressure of my grasp. That means a lot. It helps me.

We turn from the terrible sight and I try to crowd the hateful images from my mind. But though I avert my eyes, my senses will not let me forget. I can still smell the unmistakable stink of death — shit, blood, the noxious fumes which belong inside bodies, not outside. I can almost taste it in the air; either that, or the bitterness of my own impotence is polluting my body as well as my mind. And even as I cycle away, Jade walking beside me, I can hear the sounds of people dying, and corpses deflating. The sounds of the Ruin.

"What will happen to them?" I ask.

"They'll be put to use," Jade says quietly. "Things are too bad now to waste anything."

I do not ask what she means; I do not wish to know.

V

We travel a further three miles that day, taking it in turns to ride the tricycle, before exhaustion claims us. While Jade wanders off to find somewhere to camp, I wait by the side of the road in the shade of a shirt stretched across the handlebars. She is gone for nearly half an hour and I am becoming worried, but this does not stop me from falling asleep. When I wake up she is standing there, looking down at me, a strange expression on her face. I don't know whether to be frightened or excited by this unusual, confident, aggressive woman.

We wheel the trike most of the way, but for the last few hundred paces we have to virtually carry it up a steep gradient. By the time we reach the small plateau Jade has found we are both exhausted, and sleep claims us before we can erect a shelter.

I wake from a dream of cool water, innocent nakedness beside a waterfall, greenery and fruit growing all about. Jade is rubbing cream into my bare legs where the sun has found its way through the cotton of my trousers, which I see lying in a heap beside me. Before I am fully awake I see that curious expression in her eyes once more and her hands move quickly up to my groin.

Whatever stresses had been tempering Jade's attitude to me earlier that day seem to have evaporated in the sun. Perhaps it was the tension of knowing what was to come, but feeling unable to tell me beforehand. Maybe the fear that we could have fallen into trouble leaving Malakki Town had distanced her from me; after all, she has been this way before. She is doing all this now simply as a favour to me. Whatever the cause of today's tension she seems as happy now as she was last night.

The memories of the day, the trials of the journey thus far, the twinges from my chest cause me to remain limp, even as I watch Jade strip. But she works on me with her hand, her mouth, and soon we are making love under the astonished stars.

We drift towards sleep around midnight. I see a shooting star, but Jade says it is just another falling satellite.

PART THREE
THE FLIGHT OF BIRDS

i

"I'm older than you think," Della once said to me. "It's as if since losing my legs there's less of me to age; time can't find me, sometimes, because I'm not whole, I'm a smaller target than most. I'm older than you think."

I almost asked how old, but in reality I did not want to know. Her age was just another enigma, an unknown that made her even more mysterious and exotic in my eyes. She scratched her stumps as I looked around the overgrown garden; I tried to appear blasé but actually felt so nervous in her presence that I could have fainted. She was not ashamed of her terrible wounds — seemed to display them as a badge of worldliness, sometimes — but still I hated them. It was extremely disorientating looking at the stumps of legs that should continue on down to the floor. Instead, they were cut short at the edge of the wheelchair. Sometimes, when Della scratched them all night, she drew blood. I tried to get her talking.

"So what happens now?"

It was the start of the Ruin. The Sickness was still to come, lying in wait in some distant African cave like the ghost of a wronged nation ready to exact a chilling, relentless revenge. The first nukes had fallen in the Middle East, and money markets across the globe had crashed the previous month. Britain was already threatening a worldwide ban on trade, import or export. In some areas of the country, martial law had been declared. It was rumoured that people were being shot. In London, the army was hanging looters caught pillaging pickings left behind the NumbSkull plague, while the bloated bodies of the plague victims had become home to fatter, less homely pigeons than those which adorned Nelson's column.

Della shrugged, rolled her eyes skyward. "Well, you heard them, kiddo, telling everyone how good it would be. The Lord Ships are mighty fine and high, ready, they say, to restore to us all that we've lost over the last few years: justice, law, peace, even food. In the meantime, where do you think the Lords live? What do you reckon they eat?"

"I don't know."

"Somewhere nicer and something better than you, that's where and what." She flinched as her nail caught a fold of skin and opened a cut. A tear of blood formed on the stump and I watched, fascinated, as it grew, swelled and then dropped like a folded petal to the ground. When I looked up, I saw that Della had been watching me watching her.

"But don't you think it'll all work out for us?" I asked, naive and blindly trusting. "They say it's the answer. 'Government from afar', they say."

"I think the Lord Ships will last a long time," she mused. She sat back in her chair and stopped worrying her absent legs. I knew the signs — she was warming to the subject, not only because she loved sharing her wisdom with me, but also because it would stop her hurting herself. At least, for a time.

"At the end of that long time," she continued, "there're going to be a lot fewer people in the world. I think the Lords'll rule adequately, considering, but they'll also reap any rewards of their labours before anyone else has a chance to. The worst thing is..." She trailed off. This was something that Della never did; she had an angle on everything, an opinion for anyone who would listen. She stared up at the moon where it was emerging from the azure blue of a summer sky; I'm sure that for those few moments she was alone, and she had forgotten how different life had become.

"What's the worst thing, Della?" I asked. Each time we spoke, I remembered her every word, repeated them to myself like a mantra as I drifted off to sleep. They were precious to me-in a way, priceless. Some people — a few — still read the Bible; my bible consisted of Della's words.

"The worst thing, kiddo, is that they're going to be gods."

Della sent me away then, complaining about her stumps, saying her legs were aching and she could only ever put the ghosts to sleep when she was alone. I knew what she meant, but sometimes I lay awake at night, imagining a pair of discorporeal limbs stumbling along a dusty road.

I left Della to her thoughts, knowing that I would benefit from them the next time we met. Della was a treasure.

ii

I wake in the night and hear the distant sounds of engines, protesting as if hauling a huge weight up a steep slope. Lights float in the dark distance, pause for a while and then continue on their journey. Jade does not see or hear or if she does she pays no attention.

I think of the massacre, of the bodies cooling in the night, providing food for whatever wild creatures remain. I huddle closer to Jade, but sleep eludes me. The darkness is haunted by the silvery twinkle of stars, their brightness distracting and surprising at this altitude.

Sometime in the night, just before the darkness flees and there is a brief lull in nature to greet the dawn, I hear a faint sound from the south. A wailing, but made up of many voices; a harsh noise, like the tortured grind of metal on stone. I sit up and listen harder, but then the birds start singing and their song drowns the noise. I am glad.

When Jade wakes up I tell her, but she merely shrugs and smiles. "Another Lord Ship over the town."

"But I didn't hear it coming."

"Sometimes they just drift in from over the sea, then out again. Sometimes, they're as consistent as the tides."

I shake my head. "But they're not manned anymore. The Lords died, or...or fled."

Jade shrugs. When she has no answer, she shrugs.

She begins to prepare breakfast - a thick, stodgy gruel made from a paste in her bag and powdered milk, a few drops of water added to lighten the load on our stomachs. She looks tired, as if she were the one kept awake in the night, not me.

"I heard engines last night," I say, watching for a reaction. She raises her eyebrows, but she does not look at me.

I wonder whether she is beginning to regret her offer of help. I wonder how sane she can really be.

Jade does not speak for the next hour. We eat breakfast and wipe our bowls clean, then roll up the sleeping packs ready for transport. I sit for a few minutes on a large rock overlooking the valley we travelled up the previous day. The Sickness is not too bad today, the pain bearable, the growths only leaking small amounts onto my already stained and caked shirt. From my observation point I cannot make out the gulley where the bodies lie, nor the dried stream bed, nor even the wall that had hidden the terrible slaughter from our view. On the horizon, marked more by a haze of smoke than by the actual outlines of buildings, lies Malakki Town.

Jade taps me on the shoulder and informs me that we should be going. I smile, but she is as unreceptive as before. I begin to fear that she is like this because there are things to be seen today which she cannot bring herself to talk of, just as there were yesterday. The thought makes the skin over my scalp stretch with terror, but I dare not ask. I try to remember our sex from the night before, but it seems like someone else's memory from long ago.

iii

Around midday I see the first of the birds. It is high up, almost out of sight in the glare of the callous sun. It is circling in a way that induces a vague feeling of disquiet; drifting, around and around, wings steady.

"Look up there," I say. Jade stops and follows my gaze.

"Nearly there," she says.

I feel a jolt which seems to trigger a rush of blood from my chest. I slump on the saddle, slip sideways onto the hot dust of the road. A groan escapes me as the light-headedness dulls my vision.

"String?" I manage to whisper through the haze of pain.

"Just over that brow," Jade replies. I try to hear pity in her voice, but even my own yearnings cannot paint indifference a different shade. "Come on."

She grabs me under my armpits and heaves me back

into the trike's saddle. I have no strength to pedal, so she has to push me the final stretch to the top of the small hill. As we reach the summit and look down into the shallow valley beyond, I am dazzled by something in the distance. At first I think it is the sun reflecting off a body of water, and my heart leaps. Water! A wash! A bath, even! Then my eyes adjust to the glare and detail rushes in, and I realise how wrong I am.

What I do see is far more fantastic than a deep lake in an area stricken with drought.

There is a small village in the valley. The collection of tents and ramshackle huts is inconsistent with my preconceived image of String and his people, but the closer I look the more I can detect design in the apparent chaos of the scene. The whole place is pleasing to the eye — not only providing colour in a bland land blasted by winds and heat, but also offering a geometry that seems to comfort with its very order.

Around the village is a moat; off this the sun is reflected from something bright, hard-edged, many-angled. Jade turns to me and truly smiles for just about the first time that day.

"String's lake of glass," she says. I want to ask more, but suddenly feel the urge to find out for myself.

We start down the hillside and are soon approached by two guards. They are carrying guns, ugly squat black cylinders that could spit hundreds of rounds per second. They are both tall, muscular, fit-looking, their skin a healthy tan, their clothes neat and presentable. They seem to be wearing something approaching a uniform: thin cotton trousers, khaki shirts buttoned at the wrists and neck to protect them from the sun, peaked caps to keep the glare out of their eyes. They are cautious but confident as they stop a dozen steps in front of us and casually place their hands on their guns. They regard us with what I can only describe as pity, and I am jolted from the grey haze of pain that still dulls my senses.

Pity is the last thing I expect.

"You're Tiarnan, right?" Jade says. The guard on the right tenses, then nods. He steps forward, swinging his gun to bear upon us.

A sense of unease seizes me, tensing my muscles and stiffening my neck. No one knows we're here, I think. No one will miss us. There are a thousand bodies back down the road, what would two more be added to them? More food for the dogs? More human detritus to leak slowly back into the soil, replacing the goodness we've bled from the planet for centuries? I wonder if Della will miss me. I wonder if she ever expected to see me again, once I left that final time. I had the suspicion then — and it still niggles now, even though I've come so far — that she sent me here to give me hope in my final days. She never really believed in what she told me; she did not have any real faith in her words of comfort.

"Jade Kowski?" The guard's expression does not change but there is familiarity in his voice. His gun swings slightly until it's pointing directly at me.

"Hi, Tiarnan. Who's your buddy?"

Tiarnan waves a hand at the other guard. "Oh, that's Wade." He lowers his gun — but Wade, I notice, does not follow suit — and approaches Jade. "What the fuck are you doing back here, girl?" He claps her on the shoulder and ruffles her hair with fatherly affection, though I guess Tiarnan to be younger than Jade by at least half a decade; despite having a face prematurely aged by the sun and the Ruin, he has a kid's smile.

"Brought a friend." Jade nods down at me where I slump weakly on the trike. "String still entertaining?"

Tiarnan shrugs. "When people make it here. Still pretty exclusive, though, y'know?" He looks me over, removing his dusty sunglasses and squinting in the sudden brightness. At first I feel like an exhibit in a museum of dying people, but I think I detect the pity in his eyes. He glances at my shirt, muddied by the fluids leaking from me. He sees Jade's bandaged hand, notices the bright redness of the scrape on her leg set against the more subtle pink of sunburn.

"Hell, Jade, you sure ain't looking after yourself." He looks across at his companion who at some secret signal lowers his gun. "Wade, do me a favour, push our friend here down to the moat. Jade, why not walk with me? You can tell me why you're still in this Godforsaken country after all String did for you."

"You're still here," she says, but Tiarnan laughs and starts off towards the glittering moat.

Wade pushes the trike; I could pedal, but I'm tired and in pain and not about to pass up the opportunity of a free ride. When we reach the moat I can see what it really is. I wonder at the work that went into making it: the weeks of travelling to and from towns and deserted villages to collect all the materials; the dedication; the planning. The idea itself is sheer brilliance.

The moat is at least twenty metres across, and is composed entirely of broken glass: bottles, window panes, bowls, mirrors, windscreens, all smashed into a sea of sharp, deadly blades. The sun glares off its multifaceted surface and throws up a haze of light, and I can barely keep my eyes open. It is as effective as a thick fog at concealing what lies beyond.

I wonder how we will cross, but then I hear the musical crunching of glass cracking and shattering. Before I have a chance to see what is happening, Wade is lifting me from the trike and sitting me gently on a large, flat-bedded vehicle which has crawled across from the other side. Wade and Tiarnan help two other men haul on a rope, dragging the strange boat across to the inside of the moat.

"Nearly there," Jade says, bending down over me and blocking out the sun. "You okay?" As if in response pain shouts and I fade out. The sun recedes, voices float away, and I fall unconscious to the grinding sound of breaking glass.

iv

"How are you feeling?"

I open my eyes. "Like I'm going to die." It's dusk or I'm indoors; whichever, the torturous sunlight has abated.

"Well, I'll see what I can do about that." The voice is gentle, low, understated. But there is a power there, a certainty of control, a glaring confidence. Even before I see who has spoken, I know I am talking to String.

I turn my head and there he is, sitting calmly beside my bed, Jade standing behind him and Tiarnan next to her. String is a surprisingly small man: for some reason I had been imagining him huge and powerful - and another surprise is that he is black. It is only now that I realise I have seen no other coloured people on Malakki. The world is getting larger.

"Yes, I'm small, black, pretty innocuous really. I thought Jade, perhaps, would have told you about me?" He is trying not to smile, but there is laughter painted all over his face.

"Only what you can do," I say. I manage to sit up, cringing as the Sickness sends a wave of shivering heat through me.

"It's progressed quickly, hasn't it?" he says. It is more a statement than a question, so I say nothing. "May I?" He reaches for my shirt before I can object and gently pops the couple of remaining buttons. I look down as he bares my chest, and even I recoil in disgust.

String, however, retains his composure. He passes his hand close to the ugly growths and I'm sure I can feel the subtle movement of air. It is comforting. He is frowning, his big eyes so full of a pained compassion that I cannot recognise the look for several seconds. Even Della is more concerned than compassionate, an attitude which reflects her sense of realism rather than personal choice.

"It must hurt," he says.

"You bet." But I'm used to the pain, the burning that tears at my chest as if some rabid animal is trapped within, trying to escape. It's the faints I cannot conquer, the regular grey spells when my body seems to say, right, that's it, enough for now. "But the pain won't last forever."

String looks at me, then his face splits into an infectious smile. I feel myself mimicking him, and it appears that Tiarnan was born grinning. I look at Jade. She smiles back at me, but I still don't know her quite well enough to read the expression. I wonder once more whether everything bad has happened, or if there are still terrible things left for me to see.

"That's true, Gabe," he says. "Because I'm going to cure you."

v

An hour later, when I am feeling stronger, String takes me on a walking tour of the village, leaving Jade and Tiarnan chatting comfortably. It is larger than I first had thought, stretching back along the course of the shallow valley and into a ravine formed by a small stream. The waters have long gone, but the stream bed seems fertile and lush; vegetables and fruit grow in profusion. I taste my first redcurrents in years. String tells me they owe their success to the fertiliser they use.

There are hundreds of people here, going about their daily routines with a calm assurance. Although there are huts serving as meeting places or stores, most of the people appear to live in tents, either standing alone or about on old cars, lorries and buses. I see no active motor vehicle of any kind. Some of the residents throw a curious glance my way, but most seem to know why I am here — perhaps my purpose shows in my tired walk, my hopeful eyes. When they turn away, I cannot tell whether it is out of respect or simple disinterest. I wonder how many people like me they see. I ask String, and the answer surprises me more than it really should.

"Most of them *are* people like you. Or they were, until I cured them."

I become more aware of the layout of the colony, and realise that it is far more established and self-sufficient that I first assumed. The glass moat merely protects the front portion of the village, ending where sudden cliffs rise from the ground and soar towards the sun. The bulk of the dwellings and other buildings stand further back in the ravine, sheltered from both the sun and casually prying eyes by the sheer cliffs on both sides.

"We've been here a long time," String says. "We've created quite a little oasis here for ourselves. Not just one of food and water, but...well, I like to think of it as an oasis of life, a civilised enclave in a world where very little civilisation remains." He smiles sadly, and for the first time I really believe how genuine he is. "Where do you come from?"

The sudden question startles me. "Britain."

"I'm from the Dominican Republic. Ever been there?"

"No, of course not. Isn't that where...?"

String is still staring directly at me, as though he can read the constant unease in my face. "Voodoo? No, that's Haiti. Different country. Though I believe some of my ancestors were Haitians." He leaves it at that, though my query feels unanswered.

"What state is Britain in?" he asks. I cannot believe that he does not know; he seems the sort of man who knows everything.

"Britain is...dissolving." The word appears unbidden, but it suits perfectly what I am trying to say. "It's regressing. The army has taken control in many places; rumour has it there is no central government anymore." I think of my last few days there, making my way to Southampton through a countryside filled with flaming villages and ripped apart by sporadic, random battles. At first I had thought the gunfire came from by army units taking on looters and thieving parties, but then I saw that they were really fighting each other.

"On my last day there, I saw a woman raped in the street by three men. One after the other. It was terrible. But the worst thing wasn't the crime itself, but the fact that the woman stood up, brushed herself off and walked away. As if she were used to it. As if...it was the norm. Isn't that just gruesome?"

"It's a new world," String says sadly. We stroll for a few seconds, each lost in our own thoughts, most of them dark. "What of the culture?" he asks

"What do you mean?"

String stops walking and smoothes his shirt. He is not sweating; I am soaked. I wonder whether it is the Sickness bleeding the goodness from me, or whether String is so used to the heat that he no longer perspires. "The culture; the history; tradition. The soul of the place. What of it now?"

I suddenly feel sad. I wish Della were here with us; I am certain that she and String would talk forever and never become bored or disillusioned. "It's gone," I say.

String nods; I am sure he already knew. "I thought so. That cannot happen." He motions for me to follow him and we walk towards the cliff face, passing into the shadow of the mountain. He starts climbing the scree slope without pause, and I wonder whether he intends to go all the way to the top. I look up and see the thin wedge of blue sky high above, reminding me of that first day in Jade's courtyard.

"Here," he says. I look. String is standing at a split in the rock, a crevasse that could easily be the entrance to a cave. It looks like a swollen vulva, and I wonder whether it is man-made. I also ponder what is inside, in the womb of the rock, hidden in shadows. As I near String he holds out his hands, halting me.

"Gabe, Jade brought you here. She's a good woman, though I've told her before she should leave this dying place. She's too independent to join us here, more's the pity." He stands framed by the cave entrance; his skin shines in the shadows as if possessed of an inner light. I feel completely insubstantial. "I'm going to cure you. You can be assured of that, though I know that until it's done you probably won't allow yourself to believe me. But I cannot cure everyone. There's not enough medicine for the billion people with the Sickness. And there really aren't that many people whom I think deserve curing."

I go to say something, but he waves me down.

"I've already decided that you're worthy. Jade is a good judge of character. But we're only a small community, and we treasure what we have. We have to. Because we have treasures. Do you have faith?"

"Yes," I reply without thinking. He has a way of springing questions on me without warning— the way to procure an honest answer.

"In what?"

I think of Della; not only my utter faith in her goodness and knowledge, but also what she said to me. *If you know someone's faith, you know their soul...You may need it one day*. "In a friend."

"What's her name?"

"Della." I am not surprised that he knows the sex of my friend; he reminds me of Della in many ways, and she would have known.

He asks no more. I feel I am about to swoon, but String is beside me before my body can react to the thought. He grabs me around the shoulders, and his touch seems to strengthen me. I have the unsettling certainty that he knows everything about me, understands that my feelings for Della go way beyond simple friendship or even love. He knows my soul. But I am not worried, I have no fear. I think he deserves to know.

He points to the cave. "I'm going to take you in there, and show you some things. They're things I show everyone I cure, once, but never again. They're precious, you see, and precious things are coveted. Especially in the shit new world we inhabit. And ironically, that's why I'm showing you. So that you know how special what we have here is. So you know that knowledge of good things shouldn't always be shared, because too many bad things can dilute good things. Do you understand?"

I nod. Although his words twist and turn I understand him fully, and it pleases me to think that the likes of him still live on our dying world.

"I can't deny the power there is in me," he says. "You may think I'm some sort of...magician? Witch doctor? I'm none of those things. In the old days, before the Ruin, I may have been called charismatic. But now I'm a funnel for a power of a more basic, fundamental kind. The real magic, my friend, is here." He stamps on the ground, coughing up a haze of dust around his legs. He squats, grabs a handful of the dry soil and looks at it almost reverently. "The power of the greatest magic flows through my fingers with the dust." The breeze carries trails of dust from his hand and into the cave entrance, like wraiths showing us the way. "The power of Time; the immortality of Gaia."

I feel frightened, but enlivened. The Sickness sends a warm flush through me, but for once my body combats it, cooling the fever as if the atmosphere of the cave already surrounds me. String possesses me with his words; I feel no repulsion, no desire to flee. My skin tingles with a delicious anticipation. I wonder what is in the cave, but I know also that it is beyond anything I can imagine.

"This is holy ground, Gabe," String says. "I don't mean holy in the sense of religious. I don't care for religion, and have none save my own. Similarly, you have your own faith, and that's how things should be. But this site is powerful; it has a holiness that precedes any form of organised, preached religion. It has the power of Nature. It is the site of a temple, a shrine of rock and dust and water and sky that pays constant, eternal homage to Nature itself. See, up there." He points to the strip of sky between the cliffs.

I look up and see the birds there, circling, drifting on updraughts of warm air from the ravine. I sigh and feel any remaining tension leave me, sucked into the sky by the soporific movement of the birds.

"The temple is a place of faith, of worship of the cosmos. The site of a temple was often revealed by the flights of birds, their cries, their circling. As if they knew more than man about the powers of creation. And why shouldn't they? Man has long distanced himself from the truth of his creation, even though there are those who profess to seek it. He distances himself even more by worshipping gods who suit him, gods who tell him that he is set above the animals and may lord over them. Man has denied Nature; that's why he no longer knows true holiness. But the birds, now. See the birds. They know.

"This is Nature's temple. Come inside. Let me show you wonders."

PART FOUR
FROM BAD FLESH

i

We enter a tunnel. It smells damp and musty, the walls sprouting petrified fungi and lank mosses. True darkness never falls before light intrudes once more from above. It is cool deep in the rock and the air possesses something that is more characteristic of the climate I am used to — moisture. I breathe in deeply, relishing the coolness on my lungs, and I hear String laugh quietly in front of me.

The floors are uneven and the ceiling low enough in places to force me to stoop. String is short enough to walk through normally. A smell reaches us from further in, a waft of something familiar yet long-lost carried on warmer currents of air like dragon's breath. I cannot quite place the scent, but I do not feel inclined to ask String about it. He is going to show me, anyway, and for now I am almost enjoying the mystery.

Looking up, I can make out where the light is coming from — natural vent-holes that reach high up to the top of the cliff — and in doing so I miss the abrupt change from tunnel to cave. I stop, stunned by the sheer size of what lies before me.

The cave is massive. I can see that it has been hacked from the rock by crude tools, their marks still peppering the walls and ceiling like the timeless signatures of those who did the deed. It could be recent or ten thousand years old, there is no real way of telling. There are no vents in the ceiling here, but the walls are inlaid with a strange glowing material which gives out a muted light. It looks like glass, feels like metal, is warm to the touch as if heated from within. String stands in the centre of the space, smiling and staring around as if wallowing in the grandeur of whatever has been achieved here. And just what is that? What is the smell that tickles my memory once more, encourages me to silence, comforts me?

"Books," String says. He holds out his arms, indicating the hundreds of boxes stacked around the edges of the cavern. “About two hundred thousand in all. Mainly factual, though some fiction. Our descendants should know our dreams, don’t you think?”

I cannot talk. It is not simply the sight of so many boxes, but the idea of the effort that obviously went in to bringing them here. And not only that— I can’t help but imagine the thoughts and experiences which have been poured into every book here. Billions of hours of struggle, work, and strife expended on creating, writing, producing and then dragging these books through a dying world to build a library for the future. It is staggering. It is so huge that I can barely comprehend it.

String has a proud glint in his eyes, the look an adoring father gives his children. “Philosophy, biology, psychology, botany; maps, travels books, cultural works, histories; stories, poems, novels, plays; even some religious works — much against my better judgement, but who am I to choose what people will believe in the future?”

“You’ve got it all here, in your hands,” I manage to say at last. The enormity of what is here makes me slur. “You can shape the future from this place.” For the first time, I am truly frightened of String, this man whom Della had only vaguely heard of and who now holds my soul, as well as my fate, in the palm of his hand, to do with as he will.

“Not only this place,” he says. “And it’s not me who will shape it. There will be people in the future — two years from now, fifty years, who knows — who will feel the time is right. Now, to tell the truth, it’s all still in decline. I’ve merely brought these things together, protected them from the random destruction that’s sweeping the globe. It’s happened before, you know? The Dark Ages were darker than many people imagine.”

“So we’re heading for a new Dark Age?”

String sits on one of the boxes, lifts a flap and brings out a book. It is a gardening guide, sketches of forgotten blossoms decorating the cover and catching the strange light from the walls. “Maybe,” he says, “we’re already there. But when it’s over, I hope it won’t take long to get light again. I hope all this will help.”

“Who are you?” I ask. The question seems to take him

by surprise, and I feel a brief moment of satisfaction that I have tackled him at his own game.

"I'm String. I'm just a lucky man who found something wonderful. I'm doing what I can with it, because...well, just because."

"You found all this?" I say, aghast. "You must have. No man could do all this."

He shakes his head, a wry smile playing across his lips. "Faith can move mountains," he says, and I see that the saying can, in some cases, be literal. "I dragged all this here. Some I had with me when I arrived, most of it I went out and recovered. Before it was destroyed."

"I saw them burning books in the streets in England," I say quietly, the memory of the voracious flames eating at my heart. I remember thinking that the fire had always been there, waiting for its chance to engulf our knowledge and reduce it to so much dust, restrained only by whatever quaint notions of civilisation we entertained. In the end, all it took was help from us. Wilful self-destruction.

I come to my senses. "So what else is it you want to show me?"

He nods to the far end of the cavern, where another dark tunnel entrance seems to bid us enter. "I found it soon after the crash," he says. "I crawled in here to die. Then I realised I was in a very special place - had the power of life in my hands, quite literally - and the rest just happened."

"Crash?" Disparate shreds of his story seem to be fitting together; images from the last few hours intrude, as if they mean to tell me something before he speaks.

"I was a Lord," he says. "I flew a Lord Ship. As far as I know, I'm the last one left alive." He stands and heads towards the dark mouth. I follow.

ii

"Some people are not what they seem," Della said. It was cold, the chill November winds bringing unseasonable blizzards from the North and coating Britain with a sheen of ice. Thousands would die this winter: freezing, starving, giving in. The national grid had failed completely six months

previously; it had been a severe inconvenience then, rather than life-threatening. Now, though, as frost found its way into homes and burrowed into previously warm bones, the national grid was mourned more than ever. Only the week before, in Nottingham, an old theatre full of people had burned to the ground. They had been huddled around a bonfire on the stage, like a performing troupe acting a play about Neanderthal Man. The heat of their final performance melted the snow in the surrounding streets, and when it re-froze the local kids began using it as a skating rink. Surprising, how well children adapt, as if they're a blank on which the reality of the moment can imprint itself.

I handed Della a dish of curry from the vat she constantly kept on the go above the gas fire. The smell had permeated the whole house, seeped its way into furniture and carpets and Della herself. I loved it; I loved her. I never told her.

"Hm," she mumbled, "not enough powder. Next time, more powder."

I nodded my assent, hardly able to sit still with the acid that seemed to be eating away my tongue and lips. My chest felt warm; I had seen the discoloration there the week before for the first time, but I still had not told Della. It was as if telling her would confirm my worst fears to myself.

I had been told that the army was seen dumping bodies into a dry outdoor swimming pool and burning them. They'd even rigged up some sort of fuel pump, pouring petrol into the pool through the old water pipes. It meant that none of them had to get too near. I did not want to be one of those dead people, burnt in a pool, bodies boned by the flames and whisked into clogged drains.

"Take old Marcus, for instance," she continued. "You know Marcus?"

"The old guy who sits in the park pissing himself?"

"That's right, the scruffy old tramp who lets kids kick him, lies under a bench because he'll only fall off if he sleeps on it, eats grass and dandelions and blackberries and dead dogs." She nodded. "Marcus was a pilot, years before the Ruin. He flew in the Gulf War. Did they teach you about that in school?" I nodded, Della shrugged as if

surprised. "What do you think of him now?"

I could only be honest. "He's an old tramp. I suppose...I suppose every tramp is someone. Had a life before they took to the streets."

Della smiled, wiping her mouth and burping loudly and resonantly. "There you are, you see. I've made you think of him as a man, just by telling you something about him. Before, to you, he was a nobody, a tramp, someone without identity. You never even thought he was human."

I realised how right Della was. I imagined Marcus as a young boy; with a wife; going on family holidays; proud and arrogant in his pilot's suit, flying helmet under his arm as he posed for the papers. "He's still out there, and he's going to freeze," I said.

Della scoffed. "Marcus'll still be alive when you and I are dead and gone. It's as if he'd adapted for the Ruin before it happened. He was ready, his life had been a ruin for a long time." She looked at me across the candlelit room, scratching slowly beneath her chin. A breeze whistled in under the corrugated roof, making the candles flicker and Della shimmer with feigned movement. "What do you think of him now?"

I sighed. "I suppose...well, he's a tramp, but I can appreciate him. He's human."

Della nodded. "Some people aren't what they seem. Some are much more than you think, or at least better than they like to portray themselves. Some...a few...are much worse. Much of the time you'll never know which is which, but it's you that counts, what you think of them. Some people can really pull the wool over your eyes, kiddo."

I went to get Della a beer and grabbed one for myself, then sat and stared at her for an hour or two. Neither of us talked. Silently, in my own way, I was worshipping her. I wondered who the real Della was, but deep inside I had always known. She was my salvation, and I knew it.

iii

"String," I say, "where are we going? Is it dangerous?" It feels dangerous: the cool air chills me instead of comforting me this time; the darkness haunts rather than hides me. It's as if the dark here is a presence, not just an absence of light.

He turns and leans gently towards me, lowering his head and looking at me through wide eyes. They glimmer, reminding me of the strange light in the cavern behind us. "Not dangerous," he says. "Wonderful!" He walks on, then stops and looks at me again, head to one side, one corner of his mouth raised in a sardonic smile. "But dangerous if you're on your own. Dangerous, without me." He moves on.

As I follow, I speculate for a moment on what String did before the Ruin, before he took on the mantle of a Lord. But the mere idea of him existing in a normal world seems alien and abstract, and in a way it disturbs me more than the knowledge of his Lordship.

Around an outcrop of rock the darkness recedes, and suddenly we arrive at another cavern. This one is open to the sky. A great split in the rock, millions of years ago, has formed what is essentially a deep pothole, its entrance eroded by weathering so that the walls shallow out into a gully. It reminds me of a great fossilised throat, and String and I are standing in the stomach. The hairs on my neck prick up and goose bumps prickle my arms and shoulders. I have the sense of being an intruder, as if I have walked in on someone having sex or gatecrashed a funeral. But the feeling is more primal — I feel as though I have offended a god.

The gully appears empty, and is accessible only from the tunnel we have just emerged from. The floor is uneven and raised at one edge like a ramp to the walls. I can see no reason for my unease, but Della always told me that feelings tell more than sight, and I'm terrified. I assume that String's words have made me nervous and skittish, but when I glance at him he appears to be in the same frantic state. That scares me more than anything: the fact that this man who seems so enigmatic, powerful, so in control, is scared of whatever sleeps here.

"What is it?"

String does not hear me, or chooses not to. "Can you feel the power? Does it grab your skull, twist your spine? Can you sense the majesty of this place? This is the real god, Gabe; this is the genuine Provider. A god you can feel. A god who will help you, cure you." He looks at me, his eyes wide and alive, glimmering with emotion. "You'll be cured. Made better. Just like Jade. Just like all the others outside."

I want to go. Suddenly the last place I want to be is here, in this deep gully that encases me like a prison, or a tomb. But String grabs my arm and guides me to the edge of the hole, the place where the ground is ramped against the wall. I start to tremble as we approach it, and I think I can feel String shaking as well.

He hauls me up the slight incline until we are standing on a small ledge, our heads touching rock where the overhang curves inward.

I look down. There is a large stone slab on the top of the raised area, edges blurred by the scourge of time. I try to convince myself that its surface is not decorated with crude letters and drawings, but it is, and their reality will not be denied. I see mere remnants of what once must have been a magnificent tableau: half a reptilian head; the face of a god in the sun, a trail of bones; skulls crushed under wagon wheels. The words are similarly weathered, and I cannot decipher any of them. They look so alien, so unlike anything I have ever seen, that I can barely imagine how old they are.

"I think it's a tomb," String says. "And whoever is buried here must have been someone...special. This is where the power comes from."

I can feel it, an implied vibration that enters my holed shoes and seems to shiver my bones, fingering its way through my marrow and cooling everything it touches. It feels as though I am being swallowed. I want to shout, but something prevents me; it feels like a hand over my mouth, but I can still breathe. I want to run, but I am restrained;

something holds me where I am, though String is standing several steps away.

Then I can go, and I do. I turn, shout incoherently, and run. String tries to hold me, but grabs only my attention.

"Not that way," he hisses. I realise that I had been heading towards the blank, strange wall of the cave. I spin and sprint into the tunnel. The darkness seems more welcoming than the polluted light of that place.

It takes me several minutes to find my way out. Emerging from the cave is like a re-birth. The daylight is wonderful. I keep running until I am far from the ravine, almost at the moat of broken glass, and there I collapse into the dust with my face turned up to the sky, eyes closed. The sun slowly burns my face.

iv

"Did you see it all?" Jade says. There is something unfamiliar in her tone: weakness, awe. I open my eyes. She is standing over me, and moves forward to block out the sun.

"Christ, Jade, is there any more? Anything else you're waiting for me to find out on my own?" I can feel the coolness of tears on my face, soothing the sunburn that stretches my skin across my skull. I'd been crying a lot recently. It's not unusual, lately, not only for me but also for the world in general. If tears could heal, we'd all be a damn sight better than we were before the Ruin. But tears can only hurt and haunt, and remind us of our eventual, inevitable weakness.

"You saw the library? And the..." She cannot say it. I feel a sudden burst of anger.

"The what? The library and the what?" Perhaps she thinks I really haven't seen it, but I'm sure she can see way past my anger. I'm sure, in fact, that she knows all there is to know about me. I feel transparent, the same way I am with Della. Only with Della, I like the feeling. She comforts, she does not confuse.

"The tomb," she mutters.

I nod, anger draining with my sweat and tears. "Yes, I saw the library, and the tomb. Or whatever it is. I hated it."

"It's not bad, it's—"

"How the fuck do you know what it is? How do you know it's not bad?"

Jade recoils from my outburst and I revel in momentary glee at the brief look of panic in her eyes. "String healed me, Gabe. I told you, I showed you." She puts her hand to her chest, as if to hold in the goodness that had replaced her Sickness.

I sit up. "With the aid of whatever lies in there?"

Jade nods. "It's something old, and powerful. We can't pretend to understand it, just as Christians don't presume to understand God. He frightens them, maybe, but they can't ever hope to explain Him. It's like that with this place. It has something wonderful, and there's nothing wrong with using it. String has found out how to do that, and he's doing some good in the world. You know as well as I do, there's precious little of that going on elsewhere."

I begin to laugh. I stand up, feeling the fear being cooked away by the sun. Or if not removed altogether, then weakened somewhat. Fear is a strange thing when you're dying — sometimes, it seems so pointless.

"I've come this far", I say. Jade and I walk slowly back to the large tent in the middle of the settlement, a great sweeping structure held up by steel stanchions and consisting of two layers of light, soft material. The colour of the tent raises an uncomfortable sensation in my guts. Suddenly something clicks into place.

"This is a Lord Ship," I say. "What's left of the ship he crashed in."

"He used it to build the whole settlement," Jade says.

"Always thought the Lords were an evil bunch of bastards, only in it for their own gain." Della's words echo in my mind: *The worst thing, kiddo, is that they're going to be gods*.

Jade shrugs. "What you were meant to think, I suppose."

"No," I say. "No, it's something I was told." I feel an incredible sense of disquiet as I realise that my future — my life, my soul, my continued existence and well-being — now relies upon Della being both right and wrong. I hope the Lords were not all as selfish as she made them out, and at the same time, I hope that String is a god, however strange that may seem.

I wonder whether Della knew String was a Lord when she told me of him.

V

String is in the large tent, sitting at a table in the corner. The space beneath the main canopy is divided by swaying curtains of the same material. I touch it, rub it between my fingers, surprised at how light it is. It feels slick, almost oily to the touch, yet I can see through it.

"It's extremely strong," String says. "It's all that survived the crash. Apart from me, of course."

"What about the motors, engines? Weapons?"

String shakes his head. "The mechanics of the Ship burned when the fuel pile melted down. I got away before it went up. The fire didn't touch this lot, thankfully. It was built to endure. As for the weapons, that was a fallacy. The Lord Ships never carried weapons. We were a mobile, self-sufficient government, not an army." He stands, gestures us towards him. Tiarnan is already there, along with several other men and women. There is food on the table, glasses, bottles of wine and, in the centre of the table — as if in a place of honor — a large bottle of Metaxa.

"Please, sit down." String waits until Jade and I have taken our places before he sits. He turns to me, his expression slipping into seriousness for a moment.

"Tomorrow morning, I will cure you."

"How?"

"A potion. Simple. Rubbed into your chest, your temples, your stomach, it acts quickly. By tomorrow evening the growths will have hardened and dropped off. They will not recur." String hands me a glass of wine. His blasé statement stuns me with its simplicity. He is talking about my life, or my death, yet he promises everything with a confidence which makes it difficult not to believe.

I turn to Jade, who is staring ravenously at the food

arrayed on the table. "This is how he did you?"

She nods, but does not look at me. I can hardly blame her. There is more food here — in both variety and quantity — than I have seen in months. Lamb, roasted whole; a piglet, apple stuck in its mouth like a swollen tongue; fresh fruit; duckling, sliced and presented with pancakes and sauces; crispy vegetables, steaming as if to gain our attention.

"Why not now?"

String shakes his head. "Tomorrow. The power of the place is at its greatest around dawn. You'll feel it, when you wake up. You will be fresher, stronger from the food. Tomorrow, Gabe."

I am too tired to argue, and I have come too far to risk upsetting him now. I wish Della were here with me, ready with an apposite phrase or two, but at the same time I'm glad she is not. At least at a distance I can adore her fully; if she were here, my adoration would be too obvious.

We eat. We drink. The evening passes gloriously slowly, and I surprise myself by enjoying most of it. Dusk falls but the heat remains, trapped within the tent by the folds of strange material hung out like drying hides. String is a polite host, accommodating and generous with his precious food and drink. I satisfy my hunger ten fold, feeling guilty when I think of what Della may be eating tonight, but also aware that if she knew, she would be selflessly happy for me.

We emerge with the stars into the night and the alcohol flows ever more freely. String makes his excuses and disappears. Couples pair off and begin to make love shamelessly under the heavens. I see the occasional light scar on chests or abdomens, but no signs of the fully-fledged Sickness. It is like a new world. I see a flash across the horizon and Jade points it out. "Shooting star," she says.

Soon the revelry dies down and is replaced by the soft moaning of lovers, the slow movement of shadows close to the ground. Jade and I walk to the banks of the dried stream and sit amongst the fruit bushes and rows of tomatoes. The smells tempt our taste buds, even though we are still full from the meal. I pluck a tomato and bite in, closing my eyes as the warm juices dribble down my chin. I see small shadows skipping between plants, scratching on the dry ground; a lizard, as long as my foot and with glittering eyes, runs up the slight bank towards us. We sit as still as we can, waiting for it to scamper away. It waits, frozen by starlight and staring at us, before turning and walking casually back into the stream bed.

Jade giggles. It is a sound I have not heard from her, and I like it. She reaches for my shirt but I push her away.

"I'm ugly," I say. "This is a good place. I can't show my ugliness to it." I wonder if the Metaxa or the wine was drugged; I cannot help but feel fine.

"You're not ugly. It's the Sickness that's ugly, the world, the people in it. Not you." She shuffles next to me and begins unbuttoning my shirt. This time I let her. "Tomorrow, all the ugliness will be gone."

"Is there anything else, Jade? Anything you haven't told me? Is this it, is this all?" But she is taking her own clothes off now and she does not answer me. I think I see tears, but it could just be other worlds reflected in her eyes.

vi

I may be dreaming.

The ground feels solid beneath me as I sit up, the sky looks as wide and intimidating as I have ever known it. I see a dart of light streak from east to west, and wonder whether it is a shooting star or another satellite destroying itself in despair.

I hear a sound that is familiar, but out of reach. My head is light, my senses spinning. A dream, maybe, or too much wine and Metaxa?

I stand, careful not to wake Jade where she sleeps beside me. She is still naked; her skin looks grey and dead in the moonlight. I reach down and touch her just to ensure that she's still really there. She is warm, and my touch seems to imbue her skin with life.

I hear the noise again. Jade stirs, turns, mumbles something. I cannot distinguish most of the words, but I think I hear my name, and an apology.

There is movement from the other side of the stream bed. The noise quietens, and as it fades recognition dawns: the crunching, tinkling sounds were made by the huge boat crossing the moat of glass. Something has come into the camp. I wonder if I should wake someone, tell them, but then decide that whatever is happening must be a part of the camp's life. They would surely have guards out there, day and night. I slither down the bank and push my way into the mass of vegetation.

Voices reach me, quiet, muted, but obviously issuing orders. Then the sound of wheels on the dusty ground, like fingernails on sandpaper. I push through the plants, breathing heavily to draw in the smell of growing, living things. Dark shapes dart away from me, one of them scampering across my feet with a panicked patter of claws. I walk into what can only be a spider's web, the soft silk wrapping around my face and neck, and I rub frantically to clear it away. After a time I begin to think that I am lost, walking in circles among the ranks of plants, but then I reach the opposite bank. I'm surprised at how wide the stream bed is; it looked a lot narrower in the daylight.

A voice mutters nearby. I'm sure it belongs to Tiarnan, the guard who brought us in. His tone is quiet but firm, casual but confident, as if he's well used to what he's doing. I crawl slowly up the bank until I can see over the gentle ridge.

The sound of wheels begins again as I catch my first glimpse of the wagon. It is about the size of a car, a flatbedded trailer moving roughly on four bare wheels. There are three men pushing it. In the darkness, at first, I cannot make out what they are transporting. It looks like a cargo of clothes, but why three men to push it? But as the cart nears me on its journey into the ravine, sudden realisation strikes.

Bodies. Piled high on the cart, limbs protruding here and there, moving with a rhythmic *thump thump* that could so easily be the sound of heads knocking against wood.

I gasp, duck down, feeling a shout building, a scream screeching for release. But I contain it. Somehow, I hold in my terror and let it manifest itself only inside me, where a rush of blood pulses to the growths in my chest and bursts one. I have the sudden certainty that I am about to die, here, now, within sight of a strange crime and an expanse of lush plants. My breath comes in ragged gasps, as if someone else is controlling my respiration. I try to calm down, but my heart will not listen to me. I want to double up in agony, the pain from my chest sending tendrils of poison into my veins, spreading it slowly but surely throughout my body.

That's the poison from the Sickness, I tell myself, it's leaking into me and soon I'll die. And then maybe they'll add me to the cart and wheel me away, to wherever they're taking the hundreds of other meaningless corpses. I take another look over the bank and see Tiarnan standing down by the glass moat, exposed in starlight. He and three other men are lifting bodies from the huge moat-boat onto a second cart. As I watch, Tiarnan's partner fumbles and there is a sickening clout as the body hits the ground head first. He bends to pick it up, and I hear something which makes it all seem so much worse, if that is possible — a quiet laugh.

I turn and try to spot the first cart, but it has already been swallowed by the blackness. The grumbling of its wheels sounds like the gurgling of a giant's insides, issuing from the dark throat of the ravine. I wonder where they are taking the bodies. A breeze sighs through the rows of plants at my back.

It's the fertiliser, String had said.

The lake of dead bodies... the massacre I had heard and not seen...the terrible twitching of the dying as flies settled on the fresh blood... the sound of wagons that night, so near the place where Jade and I had made love and slept.

I feel sick; not just nausea brought on by the Sickness, but a sickness of the soul. I double up in pain as more tainted blood floods my system. As utter darkness begins to blank out the moon and stars, and my agony recedes into faintness, the last thing I hear is the interminable rumble of the loaded carts being pushed across the stony ground. Again, and again.

vii

Jade is looking down at me. I experience brief but vivid deja vu; is Jade my guardian angel? Her face is a mask of concern. As I struggle to keep my eyelids open she looks up, beckons someone over. I think the sky is a deep grey colour, but then realise that I am inside one of the tents.

String is here. Like Jade, he looks worried, though his eyes also betray something else, a confidence that I find strangely repulsive.

"Jade, I saw..." I begin, but though I remember seeing something terrible, I cannot recall exactly what it was.

"Keep still," she says, a quiver in her voice, "just lie still. The Sickness almost had you. String gave you the cure. Rubbed it on your chest, your temples, your throat. He thought you might have been too far gone, so he fed you some of it as well."

"Fed me?"

Jade shrugs apologetically. "A tube, into your stomach. You'll have a sore throat for a while. You were wandering around in the fruit plantation when I found you, mumbling, calling a woman's name. You looked like the walking dead."

Memories begin to force their way into the light. With them come terrible images, and an awful realisation that turns me cold.

"Jade, I saw bodies, hundreds of bodies. They're using them, storing them." I am whispering, but as soon as I begin String appears above me again, his hand lowering towards my face. I cry out, certain that he is going to silence me forever, but Jade is holding me down and String places his hand on my forehead. His flesh is cool, clammy.

"He's burning up. It's a fight, now, between the Sickness and the cure. I hope I got him in time, but...sometimes, it's a matter of will. The cure is just the catalyst."

Faintness clouds my vision, but I bite my lip and try to stay conscious. I have to tell Jade, warn her, make her get away from this place.

"Will you tell him?" I hear her ask. I can imagine her

expression: distant, worried, just as she looked when there was more bad stuff for me to know.

"Not yet," String replies. "Later, when he's better. Not now."

"I think he saw something," Jade whispers.

I sense String looking down at me. "I'll have words with Tiarnan. Stay with him, Jade. He's got a fight on his hands." Footsteps recede into the distance. All I can see above me is unremitting greyness. "If you need me, ask someone to find me. I have some work to do."

Jade bends over me again, softly telling me to be quiet, conserve my strength. And although I have some things to tell her, my body forces me to obey. I drift once more into welcoming unconsciousness.

viii

I feel different. Lighter. As if a weight, both physical and mental, has been lifted from me.

I sit up. I am still in the tent, but alone. The flap moves softly in the breeze.

Again, I wonder whether I'm dreaming. But the bed beneath me, hard and slightly bowed in the centre, feels solid. The air smells good, laden with the scents of cooking. I have a burning thirst, a sore throat. That's where they put the tube in.

"Jade!" I rasp. I can hear nothing from outside. Inside, I feel changed. I suddenly realise what is different.

I lift the rough cloth shirt I am wearing and look at my chest. The growths are crusted black with leaked blood, looking like shrivelled mushrooms sprouting from dead flesh. But I am not dead; it is the Sickness that is no more, stopped in its tracks, driven from within to shows itself as a crispy, rotten mess on the outside. Displaying its true nature.

Tentatively I lift my hand, suddenly desperate to touch myself there but aware of the pain which will inevitably come with the contact.

"Go on," Jade says from the entrance. "It's all right. Touch it. See what happens."

I look up, all wide-eyed and scared. Jade is smiling

and the expression suits her. I touch one of the growths with my fingertips, barely brushing it. It feels hard and dry, like an overcooked sausage. There is no pain, no sensation of contact at all. I touch it again and jump as, with a soft clatter, it falls off and tumbles to the ground. Lying in the dust, it looks like nothing. No threat; nothing to hate; meaningless.

Beneath the old growth there is a flash of bright pink skin. New skin.

"It'll fade to white," Jade says, moving towards me, tears in her eyes. "What did I tell you? Isn't he something?"

"I feel different," I say.

"You're better. I remember the feeling. You're just not used to being healthy. It's cleaned your blood, driven out all the bad stuff. You're cured, Gabe." She runs her hand across my chest and the growths come off, tumbling into my lap and onto the floor like a shower of black hailstones. All I feel is a slight resistance, a tugging at my chest. "You're beautiful."

I reach out for her and hold her close, crying, feeling happy and sad and scared all at the same time. "Jade, I saw something terrible."

She pulls away. "The bodies?"

I nod, struck dumb with surprise.

"Gabe..." Jade looks away, avoiding my eyes, and I scare myself by laughing. The sound reminds me of the soft laugh of Tiarnan's partner as he dropped the body, but that only makes it harder to stop. I want to hate myself but find I can't.

"Is this really the last thing, Jade?" I ask through tears of mixed emotion. "Is there anything else after this...whatever it is I'm going to be told, or see, now?"

She looks at me nervously, shaking her head. "This is just about the biggest, Gabe."

We stay silent for a while, me waiting for her to talk, Jade sniffing and wiping tears away from her cheeks. She cannot meet my gaze, her hands will not touch me. We are islands separated by a deep, dangerous sea of knowledge. I am waiting for her to let me take the plunge.

"Right," she says, standing back and preparing herself. She looks into my eyes. Suddenly, I don't want to hear what she is going to say. Out of everything possible, any words, this is the last thing I want to hear. Because it is something terrible. "Right," she says again, wringing her hands. I swing my legs from the bed in readiness to flee the tent, steal the moat-boat and make my escape before she can say any more. But String is standing in the doorway. I pause, my heart thumping; though it is forcing clean blood around my body, I find myself too scared to enjoy the sensation.

"Shall I tell him, Jade?"

She shakes her head. "It's about time I levelled with him, I think." I sit back down. Jade steps closer until we are almost touching.

"Gabe, the cure that String gave you is distilled in the presence of the tomb, under the mountain, in the realm of the flight of birds, from the brain fluid of the dead." She turns away and looks pleadingly at String.

I feel empty, emotionless, a void. I should feel sick, I suppose, but I've had far too much of that already. I'm shocked, but somehow not as surprised as perhaps I should be. I feel disgust, but second-hand, as if this is all happening to someone else. "Oh," is all I can say.

"All things must be made use of, Gabe," String says, a note of desperation in his voice as if he's trying to persuade himself as well as me. "It's a new world. If humanity wants to go and slaughter itself, then at least I can salvage some small measure of good from it."

"Did you kill them?" I ask. It seems the most important question to me, the pivotal factor that will enable me to handle what has happened, or not.

"What?" String seems surprised. He could just be buying time.

"Did you kill them? All the dead people I saw last night. Being taken into the mountain. Did you kill them?"

"No." He looks me in the eye, his gaze unwavering. He smiles grimly, tilts his head to the side. "No. You heard them being killed, or so Jade tells me. You saw them dying out there, alone, in the heat. We just use the...raw material."

"Brain fluid?" I am filled with a grotesque fascination. I wonder briefly how he knows of the cure — how he discovered it — but shove this thought from my mind.

String nods. "Yes. I won't tell you the details."

"Good," Jade murmurs. "Gabe, come here. Come here." She throws her arms around me, hugs me to her. I can feel her tears as they drip onto my shoulders, run down my chest. It feels good.

"Are you leaving?" String says.

"Damn right!" I don't believe I could stay here.

He smiles, and this one touches his eyes. "Good." He turns to leave.

"String."

He glances back, squinting either at the sun or in preparation for whatever else I'm going to say.

"Thank you."

He nods, then leaves.

Later Jade and I leave as well. The moat-boat takes us across the broken glass. I realise that I have never considered what the moat is intended as protection against; now, I do not want to know. I try to avoid standing on the darker patches in the wood, but they are everywhere, and it is almost impossible.

String is nowhere to be seen. Perhaps he is beneath the mountain, beyond the place of books in the cavern which the birds know all about. Brewing.

Tiarnan has had the trike oiled and serviced. This time, on the way back down the mountain, we take it in turns.

PART FIVE
THE SUBSTANCE OF THINGS

i

"Sometimes you'll have to put up with bad things to experience some good," Della said. "'There are more things in Heaven and Earth', and all that. Sometimes, you may not understand how good can come from events so terrible. But there are places man was never meant to see, ideas he was never meant to know. Even if it's a person doing these things, it's with blind faith, not pure understanding. Maybe that's why it's so special..."

She was in her garden again, stubbornly wheeling herself between fruit bushes, plucking those that were ripe and cleaning the others of the greasy dust that hung constantly in the atmosphere. I was following her, bagging the fruit and wondering what she was going to do with so much. There were only so many pies she could make.

"I can't see how any good has come of the Ruin. Millions have died. The world's gone to pot." I thought of the marks on my chest, slowly growing and expanding under my horrified gaze. I had still not told her. "Millions more are going to die."

She looked up at me from her wheelchair. "If you see no good in the Ruin, it's 'cause you're not meant to. Me, I see plenty of good in it."

"What! What good?"

Della sighed. I wanted to hold her, comfort her, protect her. But I knew I never could. "Look at all that," she said, indicating the basket of fruit I carried. "I'll never use all that. A few pies, a tart, a fruit salad. All that's left will turn brown, decay, collapse in on itself. Then I'll spread it on the ground and it'll give new life to the seedlings I plant next year. New from old. Good fruit from bad flesh." She took a bite from a strawberry, cringed and threw it to the ground. "So, in years to come, when all the mess of the Ruin has been cleared up or has rotted away, the world's going to be a much safer place."

I did not understand what she meant. I still do not understand now. But I like to think that she was right.

ii

We arrive back in the town and make straight for the harbour. There is a ship at anchor there, a large transport with paint peeling from its superstructure and no visible emblem or flag of any kind.

"Pirates?" I guess.

"That's all there are nowadays, I suppose." Jade has become quiet, withdrawn, but I am uncertain as to the cause. We made the journey from String's in one go, travelling through the night and keeping a close look out for roaming gangs of bandits. I'm still not sure whether I believe the cannibal yarn Jade spun when I first arrived here, but I kept my eyes wide open on the way down. Wide, wide open.

I wasn't about to be eaten after receiving a miracle cure.

"I suppose I could find out where it's heading."

"Good idea," she says. "I'll try to get us some food."

There is a subject that we are both skirting around, though I can tell by the air of discomfort that she is as aware of it as I: Where are we going, and are we going together?

iii

"When you've got a tough decision to make, don't beat around the bush. That'll get nothing sorted, and it's prevarication that's partly responsible for the mess the world's in. Remember years ago, all the talk and good intentions? Farting around, talking about disarmament and cleaning up the atmosphere and helping the environment, while all the time the planet was getting ready to self-destruct under our feet."

Della threw another log on the fire, popped the top from a bottle with her teeth and passed it to me, laughing as the liquid foamed over the lip and splashed across her old carpet. The carpet was an Axminster. I wondered what it was like in Axminster now, how many people were living in the carpet factory, whether it was even still there.

"Take that Jade. Now, whatever it is she wants she's already made up her mind, she's that type of woman. So why piss around when time's getting on? Ask her what's up, tell her what you're up to. That'll solve everything."

She scratched at her stump, drawing blood. Not for the first time I wished I could write down everything she said, record it for future reference. But somehow, I thought I'd remember it all the same.

"If there's a problem there, with you and Jade, it'll be there whether you confront it right away or in a week's time. Pass me another chicken leg."

I passed her the plate. She laughed at my retained sense of etiquette. "Manners maketh fuck-all now, Gabe. Faith maketh the man. Just you remember."

iv

I open my eyes, the remnants of a daydream fading away. I wonder how Della could have known about Jade all that time ago. I wonder how she could have known about String. I realise that, in both cases, it was impossible.

Faith maketh the man. I certainly have faith. Whether it's fed from somewhere or I make it myself, I possess it. And it possesses me.

I move away from the bench as I see a uniformed man. There is a noisy crowd on the mole, trying to get a glimpse of what is being unloaded from the hold. A few men in army uniforms lounge around, cradling some very unconventional firearms. I guess they could wipe out the town within an hour or two with the hardware they're displaying.

Hoping his uniform is not a lie, I approach the man. "Could you tell me where this ship has come from? Where it's going?"

He spins sharply, hand touching the gun at his belt, but his expression changes when he sees me. Perhaps he thinks I may have some money because I'm a European. I prepare to run when I have to disappoint him.

"Come from Australia. Go to England. Take you home, eh?" He rubs his fingers together and I back away, nodding.

"Hope so."

Jade is sitting on a wall near a row of looted, burnt shops. She has some fruit, and is surreptitiously nibbling at a chunk of pink meat.

"How did you get that?"

She smiles. "Used my guile and charm. Made promises I can't keep. Just hope I never see him again."

I frown. "Well, maybe it won't matter."

"What do you mean?" she says, but I think she knows.

"The ship's going to Britain. Are you coming with me?" There, right out with it. No beating around the bush. No prevarication.

"No," she says. I feel myself slumping with sadness. She hands me some meat, but I do not feel hungry. "Have you got someone there?"

I look at her, thinking, trying to decide whether or not I have. "Not as such," I say. "Not really. I don't think so."

"And what does that mean?"

I shrug. "I've got faith in someone, but I don't really think she exists." If you know someone's faith, you know their soul. I feel that Jade has always known my soul, and I think I may love her for that.

"I can't come, Gabe," she says. "It's not too bad here. I know a few people. I'll survive." She nibbles at some fruit, but I can tell that she is less hungry than me. "You could stay."

"You could come."

We leave it at that.

V

As I board the ship, a roll of Jade's bribe money clutched in my sweaty fist, I hear a sound like a swarm of angry bees. I glance up and see a flash of sunlight reflecting from one of the Lord Ships. It is at least two miles out to sea, drifting slowly across the horizon, but it provokes the reaction I expect.

The whole harbourside drops to its knees. Soldiers go down too, but they are soon on their feet again, kicking at the worshipping masses, firing their guns indiscriminately into huddled bodies. I search the crowd for Jade's face, then look for the alley she had pulled me into on that first day. I see the smudge of her face in the shadows, raise my hand and wave. I think she waves back.

The ship remains at anchor long enough for me to see the bodies beginning to pile up.

THE END